Dear Reader,

Within these pages you will find three uplifting stories of courage. The stories, written by some of Harlequin's most beloved authors, are fiction, but the women who inspired them are real. They are women who have dedicated their lives to helping others, and all are recipients of a Harlequin More Than Words award.

The Harlequin More Than Words program was established in 2004. Through the program Harlequin recognizes ordinary women for their extraordinary commitment to community and makes a $10,000 donation to the woman's chosen charity. In addition, some of Harlequin's most acclaimed authors donate their time and energy to writing fictional novellas inspired by the lives and work of our award recipients. The collected stories are published, with proceeds returning to the Harlequin More Than Words program.

Together with Carla Neggers, Susan Mallery and Karen Harper, I invite you to meet the Harlequin More Than Words award recipients highlighted in these pages. We hope their stories will inspire you to get involved in charitable activities in your community, or perhaps even with the charities you read about here. Together we can make a difference.

To learn more about the Harlequin More Than Words program or to nominate a woman you know for the Harlequin More Than Words award, please visit www.HarlequinMoreThanWords.com.

Sincerely,

Donna Hayes
Publisher and CEO
Harlequin Enterprises Ltd.

More Than Words

STORIES OF STRENGTH

CARLA NEGGERS
SUSAN MALLERY
KAREN HARPER

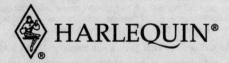

HARLEQUIN®

TORONTO • NEW YORK • LONDON
AMSTERDAM • PARIS • SYDNEY • HAMBURG
STOCKHOLM • ATHENS • TOKYO • MILAN • MADRID
PRAGUE • WARSAW • BUDAPEST • AUCKLAND

Recycling programs
for this product may
not exist in your area.

ISBN-13: 978-0-373-83668-0
ISBN-10:   0-373-83668-6

MORE THAN WORDS: STORIES OF STRENGTH

Copyright © 2008 by Harlequin Books S.A.

Carla Neggers is acknowledged as the author of *Close Call*.
Susan Mallery is acknowledged as the author of *Built To Last*.
Karen Harper is acknowledged as the author of *Find the Way*.

www.eHarlequin.com

Printed in U.S.A.

CONTENTS

JAN RICHARDSON & KATHRYN BABCOCK
⟶SHELTERNET⟵

Never doubt that a small group of thoughtful, committed
citizens can change the world: Indeed, it's the only thing that
ever has.

—*Margaret Mead*

Jan Richardson and Kathryn Babcock took
Margaret Mead's inspiring words to heart when
they first set out to create a safe Internet site to
link abused women with local shelters. From the very
beginning, Jan and Kathryn envisioned a site that
would help women across Canada—truly working
locally and thinking globally. That vision led to the
founding of Shelternet. Today, women and children,
no matter where they live in Canada, can connect
with the shelter closest to them through Shelternet.

Kathryn and Jan first met by chance when a group of women gathered to discuss philanthropic strategies. At the time, Jan was a director of a London, Ontario, women's shelter, and Kathryn was a Toronto-based corporate fund-raiser for charitable organizations. They were next to each other, and the outgoing Kathryn began to chat to Jan. The conversation turned to discussing the Internet and the glaring absence of resources out there for women in crisis. In a desperate need to find help, abused women were trying to find information in unregulated chat rooms, and shelters were receiving crisis e-mails from women without knowing how to safely respond. Shelters needed to increase their online presence in a way that would offer information and anonymity. Jan and Kathryn agreed something needed to be done. This casual meeting led to the dream of connecting all shelters for all women across Canada, and after three years of hard work and perseverance, the dream came true.

Jan has always believed a lot of important work comes into being through women's vision and passion—women dreaming the impossible and making it into a reality. "That's how women do business," Jan says. "Women network through their relationships with other women, and women show great strength in making things happen. They're undaunted—they'll champion monumental goals, and have a way of overcoming any obstacles in their paths."

With Shelternet, Jan and Kathryn had that kind of vision—to do something that had not been done before—and they had the courage and determination to realize that vision. Neither Kathryn nor Jan had a background in Web site design or technology—and they had no financial backing. But from her front-line experience, Jan knew what the site should look like and feel like to make it work for the women who needed it. The creation of the site became a collaborative effort as individuals, organizations and corporations came on board with technical and financial support.

Shelternet was successfully launched in August 2002 as the first site of its kind in the world, receiving international and national acclaim. It is available in ten languages, and Shelternet's interactive map connects women with the shelter closest to them. The site provides links to local help lines, information on developing a safety plan and stories of inspiration from other women who have left abusive relationships. Shelternet also reaches out to children and teens who have witnessed the abuse of their mothers, with special resources for them about where they can get help. So often it is children who find the information for their mothers.

The children are Kathryn's motivation for her involvement in Shelternet—and in all her work to end violence against women. It's unimaginable to Kathryn the level of fear a child would feel seeing their mother being abused. Yet in Canada alone, more than 300,000 children witness the abuse of their mothers every year. More than half the women come into shelters with children—many under five years of age. The feisty part of Kathryn can't stand women being abused and children being scared. "I wish I could be twenty-five feet tall and get the women and children out of there," she says. "I look at my relationship with my husband, how gentle and loving it is, and I want that for every woman—to never be afraid in an intimate relationship. True partnership is worth fighting for. Children raised in a loving home is the greatest gift we can give."

Jan was another motivator and inspiration for Kathryn as they worked together on Shelternet. As Kathryn describes Jan, "She had a huge history and significant experience in the shelters. She's incredibly well versed in the issues. She's extraordinary."

Jan is motivated by the possibility that a woman can be anything she wants to be, and she's dedicated her entire adult life to the experience women have in the world. But as Jan says, "That means violence. Men violate women because they can—they're allowed to." Besides having been the director of a women's shelter for more than fifteen years, Jan has served as an advocate, teacher, writer and community builder—all as part of her ongoing commitment to one day eradicating violence against women and children. Jan's work with Shelternet has been an inspiration to continue her commitment. "I've been humbled by the incredible efforts of others," she says, "particularly the rural women and shelters that have so few resources and real hardships. Yet these communities have real heart."

Jan and Kathryn believe that the spirit of collaboration can make anything possible. But as Kathryn emphasizes, "There are so many issues that need help.

Don't be afraid if you're just one person. Two is better—" she laughs "—but even one is okay. Any passion can be an issue you can volunteer for—and every skill is needed. You just have to reach out."

Reaching out is the first connection to making a real difference in a community. And in the words of Margaret Mead, it's the only thing that can change the world.

For more information visit www.shelternet.ca.

CARLA NEGGERS
⮿— Close Call —⮾

∾—CARLA NEGGERS—∾

Carla Neggers is the New York Times best-
selling author of The Angel, The Widow, Cold
Pursuit, Abandon, Breakwater, Dark Sky,
The Rapids, Night's Landing and Cold Ridge.
She lives with her family in New England.

Visit the author's Web site at :
www.carlaneggers.com.

CHAPTER
❧ ONE ❧

A dirt-encrusted mountain bike. A battered kayak. Free weights loose on the floor. Gym clothes and squash rackets hanging from a pegboard. Street and ice hockey sticks leaned up against the wall.

Brendan O'Malley's idea of how to welcome guests to his place.

As she stepped into the foyer, Jessica Stewart told herself there were no surprises. It wasn't as if she'd expected feng shui or something out of a decorating magazine. She loved the guy. She really did. She didn't know if she was *in* love with him, but that was a

15

problem for later—right now, she had to fight her way into his apartment and find out what he was up to.

Jess stuffed the key that O'Malley's brother Mike—the firefighter brother—had loaned her. Brendan was one of the cop brothers, a Boston homicide detective. The other cop brother, the youngest, was just starting out. There was also a carpenter brother and a marine brother. Five O'Malley brothers in all. At thirty-four, Brendan was smack in the middle. A guy's guy.

There was, in other words, no logical reason Jess should have expected anything but hockey sticks in the foyer.

Brendan and Mike owned the triple-decker and were renovating it as an investment property. Brendan had the first-floor apartment to himself.

Jess had rung the doorbell. She'd pounded on the door.

Taking Detective O'Malley by surprise wasn't a good idea under any circumstances, but today it was really a bad one.

He'd almost been killed yesterday.

She hoped the kayak and mountain bike were a

sign that he was still in town. Even his brothers didn't want him going off on his own so soon after a trauma.

Using the toe of her taupe pumps, Jess rolled the dumbbells aside and entered the living room. It was her first time inside his apartment. Their on-again, off-again relationship over the past two months had been at theaters, restaurants and her condo on the waterfront. They hadn't had so much as a candlelight dinner at his place.

No wonder.

It wasn't that it was a pigsty in the sense of trash and garbage all over the floors and furniture. He didn't live like a rat—or *with* rats. His apartment simply reflected his priorities. He had a flat-screen television, stacks of DVDs, an impressive stereo system, a computer, shelves of books on the Civil War and more sports equipment. In the living room.

He wasn't much on hanging up his clothes, either.

Mike had warned Jess when she talked him into giving her the keys to his younger brother's apartment. Brendan had lived on his own for a long time. His apartment was his sanctuary, his world away from his work as a detective.

Inviolable, and yet here she was.

She walked into the adjoining dining room. The table was stacked with car, sports and electronic gaming magazines and a bunch of flyers and guide-books on Nova Scotia—another sign, she hoped, that he hadn't already left.

He needed to be with his family and friends right now. Not off on his own in Nova Scotia. Everyone agreed.

Jess continued down the length of the apartment to the kitchen. A short hall led to the bathroom and bedroom. The bedroom door was shut, but she knew she'd never have gotten this far if he were on the premises. It was only five o'clock—she'd come straight from the courthouse—but he'd taken the day off.

No dirty dishes in the sink or on the counter, none in the dishwasher.

Not a good sign.

The house was solid, built about a hundred years ago in a neighborhood that wasn't one of Boston's finest, and had a lot of character. Brendan and Mike were doing most of the work themselves, but they were obviously taking their time—both had demand-ing jobs. They'd pulled up the old linoleum in the kitchen, revealing narrow hardwood flooring, and scraped off layers of wallpaper. Joe, the carpenter brother, had washed his hands of the place.

Jess peeked out onto the enclosed back porch, stacked with tools and building materials, all, presumably, locked up tight.

Brendan had mentioned, over a candlelight dinner at *her* place, that a couple of jazz musicians lived in the top floor apartment, a single-mother secretary with one teenage daughter in the middle floor apartment. He and Mike had fixed up the upper-floor apartments first because they provided income and allowed them to afford the taxes and mortgage.

Taking a breath, Jess made herself crack open the door to his bedroom.

It smelled faintly of his tangy aftershave. The shades were pulled.

The telephone rang, almost giving her a heart attack.

So much for having a prosecutor's nerves of steel.

She waited for the message machine.

"Stewart?" It was O'Malley. "I know you're there. I got it out of Mike. Pick up."

No way was she picking up.

"All right. Suit yourself. I'm on my way to Nova Scotia. I'm fine."

She grabbed the phone off his nightstand. "You left your bike and kayak."

"Don't need them." She could hear the note of victory in his tone now that he'd succeeded in getting her on the line. "Place I'm going has its own bikes and kayaks."

She noticed his bed was made, not that neatly, but he'd put in the effort. "Why sneak off?"

"I didn't want a lot of grief from everyone."

"Brendan—come on. You had a bullet whiz past your head yesterday. You need to be with family and friends."

"The bullet didn't whiz *through* my head. Big difference. It just grazed my forehead. A little blood, that's it. I get banged up worse than that playing street hockey. A couple days' kayaking and walking on the rocks in Nova Scotia, and I'll be in good shape."

"Did you bring your passport? You know, they don't just let you wave on your way across the border these days—"

"Quit worrying. I'm fine."

"You don't sound fine," Jess said. "You sound like you're trying to sound fine."

"What are you now, Stewart? Ex-cop, hard-ass prosecutor, or would-be girlfriend?"

She stood up straight, catching her reflection in the dresser mirror. Chestnut hair, a little frizzed up given the heat and humidity. Pale blue suit in an industrial-strength fabric that didn't wrinkle, repelled moisture, held its shape through the long hours she put in.

Definitely a former police officer, and now a dedicated prosecutor.

How on earth had she become Brendan O'Malley's would-be girlfriend?

"Don't flatter yourself, Detective. Just because we've seen each other a few times doesn't mean I'm mooning over you—"

He laughed. "Sure you are."

"I've known you forever."

"You haven't been sleeping with me forever."

True. She'd slept with him that one time, two weeks ago. Since then, he'd been acting as if it had been a fast way to ruin a perfectly good friendship. Maybe she had, too. They'd known each other since her days at the police academy, when O'Malley had assisted with firearms training. He was only two years out of the academy himself, but even then everyone knew he was born to be a detective. She'd been attracted to him. What woman wasn't? They'd become friends, stayed friends when she went to law school nights and then took her job as a prosecutor. She'd never even considered dating him—never mind sleeping with him—until two months ago.

She could feel the first twinges of a headache. "Some crazy fairy with a sick sense of humor must have whacked me with her magic fairy wand to make me want to date you."

"Honey, we haven't just dated—"

"Don't remind me."

"Best night of your life."

He was kidding, but she knew what had happened that night. Brendan O'Malley, stud of studs, had gone too far. He'd been tender and sexy and intimate in a way that had scared the hell out of him. Now he was backpedaling. Pretending it was her chasing him and it was all a game.

"O'Malley—Brendan—"

"I'm losing the connection. I'm up here somewhere in moose country. Quit worrying, okay? I'll call you when I get back."

"I might never make it out of this damn apartment of yours. I'll need a compass to navigate through all your stuff."

But he wasn't making up the bad connection, and his cell phone suddenly blanked out altogether, leaving Jess standing there in his bedroom, his phone dead in her hand.

She cradled it with more force than was necessary.

Bravado. That was all this was about.

O'Malley was shaken by yesterday's close call. He and his partner had entered a seedy hotel to question a possible witness in a murder, only to have the guy throw down his backpack, turn and run. An ancient .38 fell out of the backpack, hit the floor and went off.

The bullet just barely grazed O'Malley's forehead.

It could have killed him. It could have killed anyone in the vicinity.

O'Malley was treated on the scene. He wasn't admitted or even transported to the hospital. As he'd said, he was fine.

Physically.

It was his third close call that year. The sheer randomness of this latest one had gotten to him. He wasn't a target. The witness wasn't a suspect in the murder, wasn't trying to kill him or anyone else, said he had the .38 for his own protection—never mind that he was now charged with carrying a concealed weapon, possession of a weapon in violation of his probation, and assault with a deadly weapon.

Over dinner with Jess last night, after he'd been debriefed, Brendan had admitted he didn't think he'd get this one out of his mind that easily. He kept seeing the gun fall out of the backpack. He kept feeling himself yell, "Gun!" and jump back, an act that had saved his life. The heat of the bullet, the reaction of his partner, the paramedics—he remembered everything, and it played like a movie in his head, over and over.

"In the blink of an eye," he said, "that would have been all she wrote on the life of Brendan O'Malley."

He'd wanted to be alone that night.

When Jess called to check on him in the morning, he blamed his moroseness the evening before on the shrinks and too much wine and said he was heading off on his own for the weekend.

She'd talked to a few people, who all agreed it might not be a good idea for him to be alone right now. He needed his support network. Family and friends. Time to process what was, after all, a scary incident, no matter that it had a happy ending.

Not that Detective O'Malley would listen to her or anyone else.

Jess wandered back out to the dining room and flipped through the brochures and guidebooks on Nova Scotia. She'd never been to the Canadian Maritime Provinces—she'd only been to Canada a few times, including the usual high-school French-class trip to Montreal in Quebec.

The brochures were inviting. The pictures of the rocky coastline, the ocean, cliffs, beaches, kayakers, fishing boats, harbors, quaint inns and restaurants. The Lighthouse Route. Cape Breton Island. The Evangeline Trail.

So many possibilities.

How would she ever find him?

No one had shot at her lately, but Jess could feel the effects of her months of nonstop work. She'd just finished a major trial and could afford to take a few days off. She knew better than to get in too deep with O'Malley, but she had to admit she'd fantasized about going somewhere with him. She kept telling herself that she was well aware he wasn't the type for long-term commitments—she had her eyes wide-open. She didn't mind if they just had some fun together.

He'd mentioned getting out of town together for a few days. Casually, not with anything specific in mind, but it at least suggested that the only reason he hadn't invited her to go with him to Nova Scotia was the shooting. It had only been a day. He wouldn't want to inflict himself on her.

She noticed that he'd circled a bed-and-breakfast listed on a Web site printout.

The Wild Raspberry B and B.

Cute. Cheeky, even. Jess smiled to herself and, before she could talk herself out of it, dialed the Wild Raspberry's number.

A woman answered.

Jess reminded herself she was a prosecutor accustomed to delicate situations. For the most part, it was best to come to the point. "Hello—a friend of mine has a reservation with you this weekend. Brendan O'Malley."

"Right. He's not due to arrive until tomorrow."

"Thanks," Jess said, hanging up.

Of course.

He was in moose country. That meant he'd gone farther north than Portland, Maine, and wasn't taking the ferry to Nova Scotia from there. He must have decided to drive up to Mount Desert Island and catch the ferry out of Bar Harbor. He had to be booked on one of the ferries, since it would take forever for him to drive all the way up through Maine and New Brunswick.

Jess dug some more on the dining-room table and found a printout of the ferry schedule from Bar Harbor to Yarmouth, Nova Scotia.

Bingo.

If she hurried, she could make the overnight ferry from Portland, about two hours north of Boston, and maybe even beat O'Malley to the Wild Raspberry.

After he checked into a small, tidy motel in Bar Harbor on Maine's Mount Desert Island, Brendan O'Malley walked over to the cheapest-looking restaurant he could find and ordered fried shrimp and beer. There was fresh raspberry pie on the dessert menu, but he passed. Once he got to Nova Scotia, he'd be staying at a place with a name like Wild Raspberry, so he figured he'd have another chance.

He touched the bandage on the left side of his forehead, just above his eyebrow.

Man. Talk about luck.

The graze didn't hurt at all. He could take the bandage off anytime. He figured he'd let it fall off in the shower.

His brother Mike had arrived at the scene. "Brendan—damn. You are one lucky cop. How many of your nine lives have you used up now?"

"Eleven."

Gallows humor, but Mike understood. He'd had his share of brushes with death in his work. They both counted on their training, their experience, the people who backed them up—they didn't want to count on luck.

Luck was unpredictable. Fickle.

And it could run out.

Brendan shook off any hint of encroaching self-pity and paid for his dinner. He'd have to walk all the way to Nova Scotia to burn off the fried shrimp, but he settled for an evening stroll along Bar Harbor's pretty streets, not overly crowded with summer tourists. He had a reservation on the morning Cat ferry, which shortened the normal six-hour trip from Bar Harbor across the Gulf of Maine to less than three hours.

Marianne Wells, the owner of the Wild Raspberry, had assured him he'd have peace and quiet at her B and B. She only had three guest rooms. One was free, one was occupied by a hiker, and then there was the room she'd reserved for him.

O'Malley had debated pitching a tent somewhere on the coast for a few days, but Jess would have regarded that as total nut behavior under the circumstances and hunted him down for sure—or, more likely, sent someone after him. There wasn't much that could pry her away from her job as a county prosecutor. She was a worse workaholic than he was.

A disaster in the making. That was what their relationship was.

Except he couldn't imagine not having Jess Stewart in his life. She'd been there so long—forever, it seemed.

He didn't want to screw things up by falling for her.

Mike had said she'd looked worried when she'd talked him into giving her the key to his place. Brendan doubted it. Jess had been a cop for five years, earning her law degree part-time. She wasn't a worrier. She just didn't like it that he'd skipped out on her.

What the hell, he didn't owe her anything. He didn't even know how they'd ended up dating. He'd always thought of her as a kind of kid sister.

Mike hadn't bought that one. "There isn't one thing O'Malley about her. You're in denial, brother."

Ten years Brendan had known Stewart, and not until two months ago had he seriously thought about sleeping with her. Maybe she was right, and they'd both been struck by some crazy fairy with a weird sense of humor.

They'd gone to dinner and the movies a few times. Jess had dragged him on a tour of the Old North Church because he was from Boston and he'd never seen it, and that just couldn't stand another minute as far as she was concerned. But she was a native Bostonian, and had she ever been to a Bruins hockey game? One time, when she was ten. It barely counted.

O'Malley found a flat stone and skipped it into the smooth, gray water of the harbor. He had to stop thinking about Attorney Stewart. Their relationship wasn't going anywhere. They'd slept together that one time a couple weeks ago, before the shooting, but that had just been one of those things. Spontaneous, unplanned, inevitable.

He'd been such a mush, too. He couldn't believe it.

He heaved a long sigh, feeling a headache coming on that had nothing to do with the bullet that had missed his brain pan by not very much at all.

Back at his motel, he flopped on his sagging double bed and stared at the ceiling.

Nova Scotia. He could just skip it and hang out on Mount Desert Island for a few days—except the same instinct that had prompted him to jump back a half-step yesterday, thus saving his life, told him to head east. He'd been gathering brochures on Nova Scotia for weeks, checking out the tourist sites on the Internet, poring over maps, all with some vague idea that he should go there.

Maybe it was karma or something.

With his head bandaged up last night and his

brother's talk of using up his nine lives, he'd stared at the lodging list he'd printed off the Internet, picked out a B and B that looked good and called.

Now here he was, on his way. Alone.

Jess could have a point that he shouldn't be alone. "Too late."

He hit the power button on the TV remote and checked out what was going on in the world, feeling isolated and removed and suddenly really irritated with himself. But he was nothing if not stubborn, and he needed a few days to pull his head together, not just about the shooting, but about Jess.

He thought of her dark eyes and her cute butt and decided the bullet yesterday was the universe giving him a wake-up call. What did he think he was doing, falling for Jessica Stewart?

He had no intention of tucking tail and going home.

CHAPTER
~TWO~

The overnight ferry from Portland, Maine, to Yarmouth, on Nova Scotia's southwest shore, was surprisingly smooth—and fun. Jess hadn't been anywhere in so long, she made an adventure of it. When she arrived back on land, she followed the directions to the Wild Raspberry B and B, which, she soon discovered, was on Nova Scotia's South Shore, a breathtaking stretch of Canada's eastern coastline of rocks, cliffs, narrow, sandy beaches and picturesque villages.

"Forget O'Malley," she muttered to herself. "I want to go hiking!"

She'd at least had the presence of mind to pack trail shoes and hiking clothes on her quick stop back at her condo last night. Now it was a sunny, glorious morning, and she debated leaving Brendan to his own devices—his determined solitude—and finding another place to stay. He wouldn't even have to know she was there.

But she continued north along what was aptly named the Lighthouse Route and kept forcing herself not to stop, kept warning herself to stay on task. Finally she came to a small cove near historic Lunenburg, named a UNESCO World Heritage Site because of its pristine British colonial architecture and rich seafaring heritage, and found her way to the Wild Raspberry.

It wasn't a renovated colonial building like those in Lunenburg, which Jess had read about on the ferry. The Wild Raspberry was, fittingly, a small Victorian house, complete with a tiny guest cottage, that perched on a knoll across from the water. A tangle of rose and raspberry vines covered a fence along one side of the gravel driveway. The house itself was painted gray and trimmed in raspberry and white, and had porches in front and back that were crammed with brightly cushioned white wicker furniture and graced with hanging baskets of fuchsias and white petunias.

Jess parked at the far end of the small parking area—so that O'Malley wouldn't spot her the minute he pulled into the driveway. As she got her suitcase out of the back of her car, she could smell that it was low tide.

And she could hear laughter coming from the back of the house, toward the guest cottage.

Women's laughter. Unrestrained, spirited laughter.

It was so infectious, Jess couldn't help but smile as she made her way up a stone walk to the side entrance, where an enormous stone urn of four or five different colors of petunias greeted her. There was also—of course—a Welcome sign featuring a raspberry vine.

She thought of O'Malley's rat hole apartment. How had he picked this charming, cheerful place?

She sighed. "Because he got shot in the head yesterday."

A forty-something woman in hiking shorts, a tank top and sports sandals came from behind the house. She had short, curly brown hair streaked with gray and a smile that matched the buoyant mood of the B and B. "May I help you?"

"I'm Jessica Stewart—"

"I thought so. Welcome! I'm Marianne Wells. Please, come inside. Make yourself comfortable. I can help you with your bags—I just need to say goodbye to some friends."

"Don't let me interrupt. I'm in no hurry."

"Oh, we were just finishing up. We meet every week."

As Marianne turned back to rejoin her friends, Jess noticed a faint three-inch scar near her hostess's right eye. A weekly get-together with women friends—it wasn't something Jess took the time to do. Given her busy schedule, her friendships were more catch-as-catch-can.

The side door led into a cozy sitting area decorated cottage-style, with an early-twentieth-century glass-and-oak curio filled with squat jars of raspberry jam, raspberry-peach jam and raspberry-rhubarb jam, all with handmade labels. There was raspberry honey in a tall, slender jar, and a collection of quirky raspberry sugar pots and creamers.

"I've told all my friends no more raspberry anything," Marianne Wells said as she came into the small room. "You should see what I have in storage. It can get overwhelming."

"I have an aunt who made the mistake of letting people know she collects frogs. Now she's got frog-everything. Frog towels, frog soaps, frog statues, frog magnets. Frogs for every room. She even has a frog clock."

Marianne laughed, the scar fading as her eyes crinkled in good humor. "I know what you mean. It's fun to collect something, though. You must want to see your room. Come on, I'll show you upstairs."

As she started down the hall, following her hostess, Jess noticed a bulletin board above a rolltop desk with a small, prominent sign on it:

The Courage to Click. Shelternet.ca.
Shelternet can help you find a link to a shelter
or a helpline in your area.

From her experience both as a police officer and a prosecutor, Jess immediately recognized Shelternet as a resource for victims of abuse, one that Marianne Wells obviously wanted people coming through her B and B to know about.

Instinctively Jess thought of the scar above Marianne's eye and guessed she must have been a victim of domestic abuse at one time, then reminded herself that she didn't know——and shouldn't jump to conclusions.

But Marianne paused on the stairs and glanced back at Jess. "Clicking on Shelternet helped save my life."

"I'm a prosecutor in Boston. I didn't mean to make you uncomfortable. I just couldn't help noticing——"

"I'm not uncomfortable. If that sign prompts just one person to take action——well, that's why it's there. If a woman in an abusive relationship walks into this inn, I know that she'll walk out of here with that Web site address in her head. Shelternet.ca." Her smile didn't quite reach her eyes, but she seemed to mean for it to. "I don't mind that you noticed it. Not at all. I'm not ashamed of what I've been through. I used to be, but not anymore."

Jess smiled back at her. "I hope you'll tell me more about Shelternet while I'm here."

"Gladly."

They continued up the white-painted stairs to a large, airy room overlooking the water. The decor was Victorian cottage, with lots of white and vibrant accents, nothing stuffy or uptight. There was a

private bathroom——with raspberry-colored towels——
and upscale scented toiletries that surely would be a
waste on O'Malley.

Marianne pointed out the television, how to work
the windows, where to find extra linens. "My friend
Pat comes in to clean every morning. Her grand-
mother lived in this house before I bought it. I've made
a lot of changes, but Pat approves. You'll like her."

"I'm sure I will," Jess said.

"There's one other guest room on this floor and a
room on the third floor in what was once the attic.
A long-term guest is staying there. Brendan O'Malley
will be staying on this floor. He's not here yet. I
thought you two might have made arrangements to
arrive together."

Jess felt a twinge of guilt. When she'd called back
to make a reservation, Marianne had recognized her
voice from her previous call about O'Malley. "Uh, no."

Marianne frowned. "But you *are* friends, right?"

"Yes. Yes, definitely." Which, Jess thought, didn't
mean he'd jump up and down with joy to see her. But
as a survivor of abuse, Marianne Wells would be sensitive to such matters——and properly so. "We've
known each other since I was a police recruit."

"You're a former police officer?"

Jess nodded. "And O'Malley—Brendan is a detective."

Her hostess seemed satisfied. "Is there anything I can get you right now?"

"No, nothing. The room's lovely. Thank you."

"We serve afternoon tea at three, on the back porch if the weather's good, and a full breakfast in the dining room starting at seven. If there's anything special you'd like to request, please don't hesitate to let me know."

Jess debated warning Marianne that Brendan O'Malley wasn't expecting to find her here, but decided there was no point in complicating the woman's life just yet—or stirring up any old fears. O'Malley would behave. It wasn't as if he'd be really irritated that Jess had followed him.

On the other hand, he'd had a rotten week. Everything might irritate him.

After Marianne left her to her own devices, Jess unpacked, opened the windows and took a bath to the sound of the ocean, listening for O'Malley's arrival.

O'Malley waited in the hall while Marianne Wells pushed open the door to his second-floor room. The place was nice, a little quaint, probably, for his tastes, but maybe the bright colors would improve his mood. At least Marianne—she'd already told him to call her by her first name—was dressed for climbing on the rocky coastline. And the other guest, the one in the attic, was a guy.

The scar on Marianne's face looked like it was from a knife wound, but Brendan figured he was in a frame of mind to come to the worst conclusion. She could have slid off a sled as a kid and cut her face on ice.

He noticed the pink towels in the bathroom.

Pink. It was a grayed pink, but it was still pink.

He wondered if the guy in the attic got white towels.

"Your friend from Boston is in the room across the hall."

His experience as a detective kept him from choking on his tongue. "Jess?"

"That's right. You seem surprised."

And she didn't like his surprise. He could see it in her body language. She straightened, narrowing her eyes on him, and moved to the doorway, ready for flight.

O'Malley relaxed his manner, not wanting to get

his hostess mixed up in whatever he and Jess had going on. "I'm just surprised she beat me here. I thought I had the head start."

"I don't want any trouble," Marianne said firmly. "If you don't want Ms. Stewart here—if she's stalking you—"

"Jess? Stalking me? No way. It's nothing like that."

"And you. You're not—"

"No, I'm not stalking her."

She seemed at least partially relieved. "I hope not."

He pointed to his bandaged forehead. "I was in a scrape at work a couple days ago. Jess is worried about me is all. She and I go way back."

"You're a police officer, aren't you? Were you—"

"It was nothing."

Jess had been talking. O'Malley had known her since she was a recruit. She'd gone through the police academy two years after him and had done a good job on the force, but her heart wasn't in it, not the way it was in her job as a prosecutor. She absolutely believed that the system could, should and most often did work, and that she was there to get to the truth, not advance her own career, change the world or pander to public opinion.

O'Malley wasn't that idealistic. Jess insisted it wasn't idealism on her part, but a serious, hard-headed understanding of her duties as a representative of the state's interests. She'd tried to convince him of that over one of their dinners together. But he wasn't convinced of anything, except she was a bigger workaholic than he was and needed to take a vacation once in a while.

And he'd wanted to make love to her.

He'd been very convinced of that.

After Marianne retreated downstairs, he stood out in the hall and stared at Jess's shut door. Damn. What was she doing here?

The three-legged puppy syndrome, he thought.

She must have been the kind of kid who brought home injured animals, and that was what he was at the moment.

Except he didn't see it that way.

He walked over to the door and stood a few inches from the threshold, wondering if he'd be able to figure out what she was doing in there. Sleeping? Plotting what she'd do once he got there? But he didn't hear a sound from inside—no radio, no running water, no happy humming.

No gulping.

No window creaking open as she tied sheets together to make good her escape.

She must have heard him talking in the hall with their hostess.

The door jerked open suddenly, and Jess was there in shorts and a top, barefoot, her hair still damp and her skin still pink from a recent bath or shower.

"O'Malley," she said. "What a coincidence."

"Like minds and all that?"

"Mmm."

"Sweetheart, there's nothing 'like' about our minds."

But she was unflappable—she'd had longer to prepare for this moment. "I saw all those Nova Scotia brochures on your dining-room table and couldn't resist. Funny we picked the same B and B."

"You're not even trying hard to sound convincing."

She ignored him. "It's adorable, isn't it? I love the cottage touches and the raspberry theme."

He had no idea what she meant by "cottage touches." He placed one hand on the doorjamb and leaned in toward her, smelling the fragrance of her shampoo. "How's your room?"

"Perfect."

He tried to peer past her. "I think it's bigger than mine."

She opened the door a bit wider. "See for yourself."

In her own way, Jessica Stewart liked to play with fire. O'Malley stepped into her room and saw that it was shaped differently from his, but about the same size. "I didn't see your car," he said.

"Really?"

All innocence. "Did you hide it?"

"I engaged in strategic parking. If you'd arrived with a woman friend, I'd have been out of here in a flash."

He smiled. "Don't want any competition?"

"I wouldn't have wanted to embarrass you. You deserve a break, you know, after the shooting. It's just that you also need to be around friends." She scrutinized his head as he walked past her. "How's the wound?"

"I've cut myself worse shaving." He peered into her bathroom. "Do you have pink towels?"

"They're a shade of raspberry. Don't think of it as a feminine color."

"It's a cheerful place. I'll say that." He stopped in front of Jess's bed and turned to her, noticing the color in her cheeks. It was more than the aftereffects of her shower. "Now that you see me, do you feel like a dope for following me?"

"It'd take a lot for you to make me feel like a dope, O'Malley. Everyone's worried about you. What did you think would happen when you snuck off like that?"

He shrugged. "I thought I'd get to spend a few quiet days on my own in Nova Scotia."

"No, you didn't. You thought I'd follow you. That's why you circled the name of the B and B—"

"You didn't have a key to my place."

"You knew I'd ask your brother. I'll bet he okayed it with you to give me the key. Am I right?"

"Hey, hey. I'm not on the witness stand, prosecutor."

She sighed, shoving her hands into her shorts' pockets. "O'Malley—" She broke off with a small groan. "You're impossible. I don't know why I ever slept with you. My first day at the academy ten years ago, I was warned about you."

He feigned indignation. "Warned in what way?"

"Every way."

"What, that they don't come any smarter, sexier, more hell-bent on catching bad guys—"

"More full of himself, more hell on women, more cynical—"

He shook his head. "I wasn't cynical in those days."

"You are now."

"Only a little."

He approached her, slipping his arms around her as she pulled her hands out of her pockets. She didn't stiffen. She didn't tell him to back off or go soak his head. Instead she met his eye and smiled. "You're more than a little cynical, O'Malley."

"It's to protect a soft heart."

"Ha."

But she had to know he had a soft heart—he'd exposed it to her when they'd made love. He'd never done anything like that before and wasn't sure he wanted to again. He didn't like feeling vulnerable— emotionally or physically.

She was still smiling when his mouth found hers, and he could taste the salt air on her lips, her tongue. She draped her arms around his neck and responded with an urgency that told him she'd at least thought about this happening on her trip up here. He lifted her off her feet. Why hadn't he asked her to come with him? Maybe she was right and it was some kind of test, some kind of sexy game between them.

"O'Malley." She drew away from him and caught

her breath. "Brendan. Oh, my. I didn't mean——" She didn't finish. "Maybe we should take a walk."

"A walk?"

"It's a gorgeous day."

"Right."

He set her down and backed up a step, raking one hand through his close-cropped hair. She licked her lips and adjusted her shirt, which had come awry during their kiss.

"I'm on a rescue mission," she said. "I shouldn't be taking advantage of your situation."

"Why the hell not?"

But the moment had passed. She had something else on her mind besides falling into bed with him—not that it was easy for her, he decided. She just had a lot of self-discipline.

"I'll meet you downstairs," she said. "We can take a walk, then do afternoon tea."

That was it.

Jess made her way to the door and held it open for him as he strode past her back out into the hall. "Think Marianne Wells would have a ham sandwich or something at tea time?"

"I doubt it."

"Little scones, probably, huh?"

Jess smiled, looking more at ease, less as if she was afraid he'd go off the deep end at any moment. "I'd count on something with raspberries."

The afternoon stayed warm and sunny, and Marianne served tea on the back porch, laying out an assortment of miniature lemon scones with raspberry jam, tiny triangles of homemade bread, fresh local butter and watercress, and warm oatmeal-raisin-chocolate-chip cookies that one of her friends had dropped by that morning.

Jess couldn't have been happier, but O'Malley looked a little out of place sitting on a white wicker rocker with a watermelon-colored cushion as he negotiated a Beatrix Potter teacup and plate of goodies.

He'd gotten rid of the bandage on his forehead. His bullet graze looked more like a nasty cat scratch. Probably no one would guess what it really was, or even bother to ask. He'd had no trouble negotiating their hike along a stunning stretch of the rugged granite coastline. Whenever the afternoon sun hit his dark hair, his clear blue eyes, Jess was struck again by how really good-looking and madly sexy he was. She hadn't thought about his mental state—the possibility he was suffering from post-traumatic stress symptoms—at all.

Maybe it was being away from Boston—violence and his work seemed so far removed from Nova Scotia.

Or maybe it was the way he'd kissed her.

When a middle-aged man joined them on the porch, Jess forced herself to push aside all thought of kissing Brendan O'Malley.

The man introduced himself as John Summers, the Wild Raspberry's third guest. He had longish graying hair and a full gray beard and was dressed in worn hiking shorts and shirt, with stringy, tanned, well-muscled legs and arms. He looked as if he'd been strolling the nooks and crannies of Nova Scotia for months, if not years. His eyes were a pale blue, and he had deep lines in an angular, friendly face.

But something about him immediately set off O'Malley's cop radar. Jess could see it happening. He started with the inquisition. "How long have you been here?"

"A month. Gorgeous spot, isn't it?"

"Sure is. Spend the whole month here alone?"

Summers winced visibly at O'Malley's aggressive tone, then said coolly, "As a matter of fact, yes."

"Must be relaxing. Hike a lot? Or are you into sailing?"

"Hiking and kayaking, mostly." He sat on a wicker chair with his plate of goodies and a cup of tea and changed the subject. "What brings you to Nova Scotia? You're American, aren't you?"

"From Boston. Just taking a few days off." O'Malley didn't take the hint and back off. "Where are you from?"

"Toronto."

"That's a ways. You fly here or drive?"

Jess tried to distract O'Malley from the scent by offering him a warm cookie. He didn't take the hint. Summers, to his credit, just answered the question. "I flew into Halifax."

"I've never been to Halifax," Jess said.

Summers seized on her comment like a lifeline. "It's a wonderful city. I hope you'll have a chance to spend a day there, at least, while you're here. The entire South Shore is worth seeing. Lunenburg can occupy you for quite some time."

"What would you recommend I see?"

O'Malley scowled at her as if she'd interfered with a homicide investigation. He said nothing, just downed a final scone in two bites. Jess chatted with their fellow guest about South Shore sites, then got him to recommend hiking trails. O'Malley finally growled under his breath and excused himself.

Summers nodded at his retreating figure. "You two know each other?"

"We work together," Jess said vaguely. It was close enough to the truth. "He had a bad experience before coming up here."

"He reminds me of a cop. Are you two in law enforcement?"

Jess sighed, then smiled. "Caught. Brendan's a homicide detective. I'm a prosecutor."

He didn't seem pleased that he'd guessed right. "Have you prosecuted many domestic abuse cases?"

"Too many on the one hand, too few on the other."

"Meaning domestic violence shouldn't happen, ever, but it does and you want to get all the perpetrators." Summers nodded with understanding. "Our hostess left an abusive marriage two years ago. She's a very courageous woman. She's come a long way in a relatively short time."

Jess set her plate down, no longer hungry. "The scar above her eye?"

"Her ex-husband's handiwork. He was convicted. He's out of prison now. He was a businessman in Halifax, but he's relocated to Calgary." Summers's expression didn't change, but Jess could feel his sarcasm. "Apparently he said he needed a fresh start."

"Not for her sake, I'll bet."

"He's from western Canada originally. His reputation here was in tatters. People didn't want to believe he was capable of abuse, but the knife cut ended their denial."

Jess wondered why he was telling her all this. "It looks as if Marianne's built a new life for herself."

"She has. It wasn't easy. She told me she used to worry constantly that he'd come back. On some level, I think she still does."

"The emotional wounds of abuse can take a long time to heal."

He looked away. "Sometimes I wonder if they ever do, if someone who's been through that kind of horror can love and trust someone again——" He broke off, as if he hadn't meant to go that far, adding sharply, "Marianne has put all she has—her time, her money, her energy, her love—into getting this place up and running, into her life here. She has friends, she volunteers at a local shelter."

Something about his manner struck Jess as antagonistic, even accusatory. "Mr. Summers, we're not here to upset anyone—"

"What happened to your friend Detective O'Malley? He's had a recent brush with violence, hasn't he?"

"You're very perceptive. It wasn't a major incident, fortunately."

"But it wasn't the first. Men like him—" Summers paused, seeming to debate the wisdom of what he wanted to say. "They're magnets for violence."

"Not O'Malley," Jess said, although she didn't know why she felt the need to defend him.

Summers looked past her. "I've been her only guest on and off since I arrived, especially during the week. Weekends she's usually full." But he had a distant look in his eye, as if he wouldn't necessarily trust himself—or maybe Jess was reading something into his manner that wasn't there because of

O'Malley's instant suspicion of him. Summers drifted off a moment, then smiled abruptly. "I'm sorry. I don't mean to be rude."

"You're not the one who was rude."

He almost laughed. "Well, I suppose we want a homicide detective to be of a suspicious nature. Does he give everyone the third-degree like that?"

"Actually, no. I think he's just on edge."

"It's taken a lot of courage and effort for Marianne to build a life for herself that's free of violence. See to it he keeps himself in check, okay?"

"Mr. Summers, Brendan has never lost control—"

"I'm sure he hasn't." He made a face, rubbing the back of his neck as he heaved a sigh. "And I'm sure Marianne would have a fit if she thought I was protecting her. She can take care of herself. She has a great group of friends. She's one of the most positive people I've ever met."

Jess smiled at him. "Smitten, are you, Mr. Summers?"

His cheeks reddened slightly. "I guess there's no point in hiding it."

"She's not interested?"

He shook his head. "I wouldn't know. I haven't—"

He frowned suddenly. "You must be a hell of a prosecutor, Ms. Stewart. I didn't mean to tell you any of this."

"Call me Jess," she said. "And, yes, I do okay in my work."

She joined O'Malley in the English-style garden, filled with pink foxglove, purple Jacob's ladder, pale pink astilbe, painted daisies, sweet William, lady's mantle and a range of annuals. He looked as if he could stomp them all into the dirt. Jess inhaled deeply. "I could get into gardening."

"The guy's lying about something."

"Oh, come on. You don't know that."

He mock-glared at her. "Your gut's telling you the same thing."

"Maybe, but not all untruths are nefarious untruths. What set you off?"

"He's been here a month, shows up looking like he could scale the Himalayas. This isn't your 'outdoors guy' kind of place."

Jess smiled, amused. "Because of the pink towels?"

"You know what I'm saying."

"No, I don't. You're here—"

"That's karma or something. I can't explain it." He

grimaced, as if the thought of trying to explain how he'd ended up at the Wild Raspberry made him miserable. "Whatever Summers is hiding, it's more than a social lie."

"Like telling me you're staying home in bed when you're actually packing for Nova Scotia?"

"That was a strategic lie. I knew you wouldn't leave me alone otherwise." He had a sexy glint in his eyes that he seemed able to produce at will. "You didn't, anyway."

"You can be alone after you're over the shooting."

"I was over the shooting once I knew the bullet missed."

Jess didn't argue with him and instead related her conversation with their fellow guest. O'Malley looked disgusted. "I hate wife-beaters. I knew a guy my first year on the force who beat up his wife and kids. He was a good cop. No one wanted to believe it, but it was true."

"What happened to him?"

"He went through anger management—after his wife packed up herself and the kids and got out of there before he could do more damage. He lost his job. He screwed up a lot of lives, including his own, before he figured out he was the one who had to change. Most guys don't ever figure that out. It was an eye-opener for the rest of us, seeing that a guy we respected was capable of beating up on his wife and kids."

Jess glanced back at the porch. "If Summers has a thing for Marianne and has lied——"

"She's not going to like it."

"He seems to admire her a great deal."

"Maybe." O'Malley tilted his head back and smiled. "The sun and sea agree with you, Stewart. You're looking good this afternoon."

"I wish I could say the same for you."

"I don't look so good?"

"No. You look like you had a bullet whiz past your head a couple of days ago."

He shrugged. "You still think I'm sexy."

"Where did you get the idea——"

"Uh-uh. You can't take it back. I heard you whisper it when we were in the sack——"

"Not so loud!"

He grinned broadly. "Shy?"

"I just don't need to be reminded. You're the lone-wolf type, O'Malley. Two seconds with you, and people know it."

"Lone-wolf type? What the hell's that? I like women."

"My point, exactly. Women. Plural."

He stared at her as if she'd just turned chartreuse.

"I don't want to fall for a guy like that," she told him.

"Hey. Lone-wolf. A guy like that. I think I'm being categorized here. You're not the only one who did some talking that night—"

"Yours was just of the moment. You were pretending to be what I wanted you to be."

He stared at her. "Stewart, where are you getting this stuff?"

But after his recent brush with death, Jess didn't want to get into an intimate, emotional talk with him. She didn't regret their night together, but she'd made the mistake of letting him know that she was attracted to him on a level that just wasn't smart. He'd responded in kind, but she knew better than to take what he'd said to heart.

No wonder he'd run off to Nova Scotia.

She squared her shoulders. "I followed you up here as a concerned colleague, nothing more."

"Uh-uh." He sounded totally disbelieving. "You didn't kiss me like a concerned colleague—"

"Well, you'd been shot at. I thought I could indulge you that once."

"It was a charity kiss?"

"Something like that."

He grinned at her. "Then I'll have to figure out a way to get another."

CHAPTER
◦~ THREE ~◦

O' Malley dragged Jess out for dinner and
a scenic drive through beautiful Lunenburg with its restored historic houses,
narrow streets and picturesque waterfront, then on
along the coast, past lighthouses and coves and cliffs.
When they arrived back at the Wild Raspberry, Jess
found a book in the library and settled on the front
porch. She looked content, not so worried about
him. O'Malley felt less jumpy, less as if he could—
and should—run clear across Canada and not come
up for air until he got to Vancouver.

Not that the dark-eyed Boston prosecutor on the front porch had a calming effect on him.

Suddenly agitated, he stormed down the steps and walked across the road to the water. The tide was going out, seagulls wheeling overhead, a cool breeze bringing with it the smell of the ocean. The sun had dipped low on the other side of the island, and dusk was coming slowly.

He spotted Marianne Wells sitting on a large boulder, her knees tucked up under her chin, her arms around her shins as she stared out at the Atlantic. Not wanting to disturb her solitude, he veered off in the other direction, heading down to a shallow tide pool forming amidst the wave-smoothed rocks as the water receded.

"Detective O'Malley?" Marianne jumped up off her boulder and trotted down to him, her agility on the rocky shore impressive. He paused, waiting for her to catch up to him. "I was wondering if I could talk to you about something."

"Sure. What's up?"

She didn't jump right in with what was on her mind, but nodded at the tide pool. "It's amazing—it never changes. I've come out here every day since I got here. I had the house, friends—hope. I'm one of the lucky ones."

"I understand you're a survivor of domestic abuse."

"My husband started out by isolating me from my family and friends. He worked on my self-esteem, belittling me, telling me I was ugly, stupid, going into rages when I made even the tiniest mistake—" She took a breath, but didn't look away from him. "He didn't hit me at first. That came later."

"How long were you with him?"

"We met a year before we married. We were married for seven years."

"No children?"

She shook her head. "That helped when it came to making a clean break with my abuser. Visitation access often becomes another way for abusers to continue to control women. And children…what they see, their own lack of control…"

"It's a vicious cycle," O'Malley said.

"I gave up a lot when I decided to do something about my situation. There's no denying that I didn't. It's not just challenging the violence that takes courage, but deciding to give up the status quo and embrace an uncertain future."

"I've been to too many domestic-abuse crime scenes. Are you worried this guy'll come back?"

"A tiny bit less with each day he doesn't. I'm prepared for that fear to go on. I've found ways to live with it. I have a lot of support."

"You've done a good job with your place here."

She smiled, but without looking at him. "I didn't think I could do it. I thought I'd fail. A part of me believed he was right about me. But I got up each morning, and I did what I could. Then I got up the next morning, and I did a little more. Bit by bit, it came together."

"You deserve a lot of credit."

"Taking that first step was so scary and difficult. I was in the local library—I thought if I could go online and find some information, maybe it'd help." She crossed her arms on her chest, against the breeze. "I found the Shelternet Web site. It has a clickable map of Canada with links to local shelters, detailed information on how to make a safety plan, stories of other abused women. I sat there and read every word."

"How long before you went to a shelter?"

"A month. Abuse—it does things to your head."

"But you did it," O'Malley said.

She ran the toe of her sandal over a hunk of slimy seaweed. "My life was as big a wreck as this place was when I bought it. But I was living a violent-free life. That gave me such hope, such energy. It still does. I'm taking care of myself for the first time in a very long time. That matters."

"It matters a lot."

"I'd always dreamed of opening a bed-and-breakfast on the coast. I love it out here. I live in the guest house— it's perfect for me—and have the house for guests. That might change one day, or it might not. I'm just enjoying the moment. And I've done exactly what I want with the place." She let her arms fall to her sides. "I decided— I like pink. Raspberry, watermelon, orange-pink, petal pink. I didn't have to explain it to anyone or excuse it or pretend I liked chartreuse or rust when I like pink."

O'Malley smiled at her. "I'm not as big on pink as you are."

She laughed. "I appreciate your honesty. Anyway, I don't mean to bore you—"

"You're not boring me," he said sincerely.

She angled a look at him. "That's why you do police work, isn't it? Because you like people, you like to figure them out?"

"My father was a cop. I knew the work suited me."

"Jessica? She says she was a police officer, too."

"For a few years."

"Her father—"

"Investment banker. Very white bread. Her mother is a volunteer for a bunch of different charities. They almost had a heart attack when she got accepted to the police academy."

"But they supported her decision? They didn't try to stop her?"

"They were the proudest parents at her graduation."

"Good for them."

O'Malley knew Marianne hadn't joined him at the tide pool to chitchat. "Look—"

"I think someone's snooping on me," she blurted.

"What do you mean, snooping? Spying? Stalking you?"

She shook her head. "Nothing that overt. There've been these odd incidents." She took a breath, not going on.

"Like what?" he prodded.

She squatted down, dipping a hand into the cold water, her back to him. "I don't imagine things. I don't make things out to be worse than they are. The fears I have—they're real fears."

"You think your ex-husband is in the area?"

"Let's say I fear it."

But she didn't go on, seemed unable to. O'Malley walked around to the other side of the tide pool and squatted down, noticing that she had grabbed something from the bottom of the pool. "What do you have?"

"Starfish," she said, and smiled as she lifted it out of the water and showed it to him. "I used to love to collect things from tide pools when I was a little girl. I'd put everything back, of course. Once—once I forgot, and I was mortified for days."

A sensitive soul. "I understand."

Her eyes met his, just for an instant, and she replaced the starfish back in the water. "When I got up this morning, before you and Jessica arrived, I was positive someone had been through the Saratoga trunk in the living room during the night. It's an antique, from my great-grandmother."

"The living room's open to guests?"

She nodded. "But no one—it was just John Summers here last night. And he wouldn't be interested in the contents of an old trunk. He's a hiker.

He goes out every day for hours. He pays me extra to load up his daypack with lunch and snacks."

"What's in the trunk?"

"Nothing of any value to anyone but me. Family photo albums and scrapbooks of my life before I married." She spoke clearly, directly, without any hint of trying to hide something. "Some old books and diaries."

"Your diaries?"

"Oh, no. My great-grandmother's. She and my great-grandfather came to Nova Scotia from Scotland."

"Have you read her diary?"

"Bits and pieces. It feels like prying, frankly."

O'Malley shrugged. "That's half of what I do for a living. What made you think someone had been in the trunk? Was the latch open, something like that?"

"It was moved and——" She thought a moment as she got to her feet. "I'd draped a throw over it last night. It was on the couch this morning."

"Maybe Summers couldn't sleep and came downstairs to read for a while, get a change of scenery, and used the throw to keep his feet warm."

"It's possible." She smiled. "I like that theory."

"Any other incidents?"

"A few more like that."

"All with personal items?"

"Yes."

"Nothing that'd tempt you to call the police?"

"No, not yet. I just feel—I don't know how to describe it. Like somebody's looking for something, prying into my life, or if not my life, my family's past. It's a very strange feeling."

"Anything exciting about your family's past?"

She frowned at him. "What do you mean?"

"I don't know. Was one of your ancestors secretly married to the Prince of Wales or something?"

"Oh, no, no, nothing like that."

"But like something else?"

"Well—" She shook her head, laughing a little. "My great-grandmother lived in this area during a famous, tragic incident when a Halifax heiress ran off with a no-account foreign sailor. Irish, I think. Their boat went down in a storm just beyond the cove here."

"They were killed?"

"Drowned."

"Bodies recovered?"

Marianne nodded sadly. "There are rumors the

heiress had taken gold coins and jewels with her, as a nest egg for her new life."

O'Malley watched her expression and, from long experience, knew there was more to the story. "No sign of them?"

"It depends on whom you believe."

Vague answer, but he didn't push.

"None of this is like my ex-husband. He's more the type to take a baseball bat to the kitchen because I left a coffee filter in the sink. But I haven't seen him in two years. I don't know—" She left it at that, then said abruptly, "I'll walk back to the house with you. Would you and Jessica care for some blueberry wine? It's made by a local winery. It's quite good."

O'Malley winked at her. "So long as it's not raspberry wine."

She laughed again, seeming more relaxed now that she'd told someone about her snooper. He wanted to know what she was holding back, but he doubted he'd get it out of her tonight. Marianne Wells was a direct, strong, self-contained woman, comfortable in her own skin. He wondered how much of that had been there before her husband went to work on her, and how much she'd had to get back, rediscover and build after she got him and his violence out of her life.

When they crossed the road, she paused at the base of the porch steps, then turned abruptly to him. "It's all too easy, isn't it?"

"What?"

"To hide yourself from the truth. I pretended for such a long time that I wasn't living the life I was living."

"Well, you know what they say."

"What's that?"

"Denial isn't just a river in Egypt."

"Oh, stop. Oh—oh, that is so lame!" She called up to the porch. "Jessica, your friend here is just *awful.*"

Jess slid off her swing and stood at the top of the steps, the evening light catching the lighter streaks in her hair. O'Malley had tried to pretend she wasn't as beautiful as she was. Talk about hiding from the truth. She grinned at him and Marianne. "Is he telling you stupid jokes?"

"Close. Very lame pearls of wisdom."

Jess winced, still grinning. "That's our Detective O'Malley. He's got a saying for every occasion. His brothers are the same. They can reduce complicated issues and emotions to soundbites."

"Well," Marianne said cheerfully, "I guess it's a gift."

She trotted up the steps, a lightness in her gait that hadn't been there before, and went inside to fetch the blueberry wine.

O'Malley joined Jess on the porch. "Where's Summers?"

"He turned in early. What were you and Marianne talking about?"

"Violent men, snoops and treasure lost at sea."

"I hate the idea of violent men. Snoops can go either way. Treasure lost at sea—now, that could be fun."

"I'll tell you all about it. Speaking of snoops, how'd you like my apartment yesterday?"

"No vermin. That's something."

"No interior decorator, either." He moved in closer to her, smelling the scented soap she'd used in the shower. "It's a shame we're paying for two rooms."

"O'Malley—" She blew at a stray lock of hair that had dropped onto her forehead. "Damn."

"Hot all of a sudden, huh?"

"It's too late not to pay for both rooms…"

"We could do Marianne a big favor and pay for both rooms, but only actually use one. Save her on cleaning, anyway."

"You're just looking for distractions."

"It was your idea to come up here and become one."

But before she could respond, their hostess arrived on the porch with three glasses and an open bottle of blueberry wine.

Jess woke up very early and wandered outside to catch the sunrise, thinking of the rest of the continent still shrouded in darkness as the first morning rays skimmed the horizon and glowed orange on the ocean. Fishing boats puttered across the mirrorlike water, leaving a gentle wake, the quiet and stillness disturbed only by a few seagulls.

She'd never been anywhere more beautiful, and yet she couldn't relax.

It was O'Malley, of course. She'd dreamed about him.

Not good. An intelligent woman had no business dreaming about a Boston homicide detective with a penchant for getting himself shot at. Never mind all the other reasons. The tight-knit family where she would always be a stranger, the lone-wolf apartment that showed no sign of needing anyone to share it, the dedication to the job that bordered on obsession.

Then again, those could be the same reasons he was avoiding getting more involved with her. She thought of her own family, her own apartment, her own dedication to her job.

But she'd never been shot at, even during her five years on the police force.

She'd also never been more comfortable with anyone than she was with Brendan O'Malley.

Taking a deep breath, Jess pushed all thought of him out of her mind and focused on the sunrise as she walked down to the water's edge. It was just before low tide, which only added to the stillness, the sense of solitude and isolation.

When she returned to the Wild Raspberry, Marianne was up, humming as she worked in the kitchen. Jess called good morning, startling her. Marianne jumped, clutching her heart as she turned, recognized her guest, and collapsed against the counter. "I didn't realize you were up. Everything's all right? I'm fixing breakfast—"

"Everything's fine," Jess said. "Don't let me disturb you."

"It's no problem."

But Marianne's skin was pale—paler than it should

have been. She must be used to guests getting up at different hours. Jess found herself lingering in the kitchen doorway. "Marianne? Are you okay? Is something wrong?"

John Summers appeared behind Jess in the hall. "What's going on?" he asked, immediately attuned to Marianne's tension.

"Nothing, I hope," Jess said. "I was out for a walk and startled Marianne when I came in."

Marianne turned quickly. "It happens sometimes," she mumbled, dismissing the subject as she busied herself pulling pots and frying pans out of a low cupboard.

Summers started to say something, then changed his mind and stalked out to the dining room. He sat at the smallest of three tables, snatched up a Halifax newspaper and held it up, a none-too-subtle way to cut off conversation. Jess didn't know if she'd annoyed him or he just wasn't a morning person.

She helped herself to a bowl of cut fruit—including raspberries—that Marianne had already put out on a sideboard. The breakfast room was as quirky and cheerful as the rest of the house, done in yellows and blues with raspberry accents. Summers's grumpiness was out of place.

Sitting at the farthest table from him, Jess decided to confront him. "Mr. Summers—"

He sighed audibly, folded his newspaper and set it on the table. "Something's wrong with Marianne. She's on edge. She wasn't like that when I first arrived."

Given Marianne's personal background and her talk of snoops and treasure with O'Malley, Jess was especially interested in Summers's observation. "How long has she been on edge?"

"A week or so." He eyed Jess a moment, as if she were responsible for their hostess's mood, then sighed again. "I'm sorry. I wanted to blame you and your cop friend, but she's been jumpy since before you two arrived."

Jess could understand his desire to blame her and O'Malley. A cop and a prosecutor could remind an abuse survivor of her past, dredge up fears and inse-curities she thought she'd put behind her. It would make Marianne's uneasiness easier to explain. But it wasn't the case.

"You've been here a while," she said. "Any idea what's going on?"

Summers didn't answer at once, then lurched to his feet, muttering, "I hope it's not me."

Not one to let a comment like that go, Jess leaned back in her chair, chose a fat raspberry from the top of her fruit and watched Summers's stiff back as he grabbed a small glass bowl. "Why would it be you?" she asked.

He glanced over at her. "I've been here too long."

"Hiking?"

"I think of it as exploring."

He loaded up his bowl with fruit and took it out to the back porch without a word.

O'Malley came downstairs and sat across from Jess. He was showered and dressed, but he hadn't shaved, which didn't help her already supercharged reaction to him. The dark stubble on his jaw somehow made the scar forming on his forehead from the bullet graze stand out even more.

She pushed her bowl toward him. "Help yourself. I got too much."

"What's with Summers? Doesn't like to talk to people in the morning, or did you irritate him?"

"Perhaps both." But she told O'Malley about Marianne and Summers's reaction to her jumpiness, then added, "I wonder if something *is* going on around here. Do you think the ex-husband could be back? Abusers generally don't respect law and authority. And they don't like to give up. He could have got to thinking about her, found out what a success she's made of this place and decided to come back and resume control over her and her life."

"It's possible."

"But you don't think so." Jess sighed. "Neither do I."

"Maybe Summers and Marianne have a thing for each other and don't know what to do about it." His dark eyes lifted to Jess. "Sound familiar?"

"I don't have a *thing* for you, O'Malley."

"Uh-huh."

"Don't give me that dubious tone—and stop with the sexy twitch of the eyebrows."

"I had an itch."

"Ha."

"You just think everything I do is sexy."

It was true, but she wasn't about to tell him that. "We're friends. We let our friendship get out of hand. Insisting I'm falling for you is just another way for you to avoid dealing with the real issue."

"Which is what? That I almost got my head blown off the other day?"

She bit off a sigh. "Bravado, bravado, bravado."

"Yeah, yeah, yeah. Tell me more about Summers."

"He's tense, he's abrupt and he's more on edge than our hostess."

"Who is making up a hell of a breakfast this morning from the smell of it."

"Brendan—"

"I have no authority in Canada. Neither do you. If we have reason to suspect something's going on, we can call the local police, just like anyone else. That's it."

"You still think the guy's hiding something?"

"Yep." O'Malley held a raspberry up to one eye and examined it as if it were a diamond. "I think there's a worm in it."

"There is not—"

He popped it into his mouth and grinned at her. "Let's hope you're right. What do you want to do today? Go kayaking, or discuss my post-traumatic stress symptoms?"

"Both."

"Can't do both. What else?"

Jess lowered her voice. "I thought we might sneak up to the attic—"

"And search our fellow guest's room? You're going to get us arrested."

But she could tell he'd already thought of it, too. "Not if we're right and he's hiding something."

Summers returned from the porch in a moderately better mood, and Marianne set out an enormous breakfast of scrambled eggs, sausage, bacon, grilled tomatoes, corn muffins, streusel muffins and jam. Marianne's friend Pat, who also did the cleaning, had made the muffins. There was coffee, tea, juice and hot chocolate. Jess figured if she ate even a little of everything, she'd have to do a lot of kayaking to burn up the calories.

Hiking up the steep stairs to the attic wouldn't hurt, either.

When Summers retreated to his room after breakfast, O'Malley and Jess postponed checking out their fellow guest and instead went kayaking. Marianne provided all the equipment they needed—kayaks, paddles, life vests, emergency whistles, dry packs— and suggested several scenic routes that would take them anywhere from a couple hours to all day. O'Malley picked one that would have him in a restaurant, eating fresh scallops and drinking beer, by lunchtime.

After watching Jess drop her behind into the cockpit of her kayak and paddle two strokes, he forgot all about the scallops and beer and started looking for a secluded beach.

She seemed to sense his thoughts as they made their way along the shallow, rocky shoreline. "It's a romantic spot, isn't it?"

"Sure is."

"Is that why you picked it?"

"Jess, I came up here alone. I had lobster and scallops on my mind—a few days on my own, not romance."

She gave him one of her mysterious smiles. "I don't believe you."

"You think I had you in mind?"

But she stroked hard, pushing her boat ahead of him, and he cursed himself for being so obtuse. He held back, noticing the play of muscles in her arms and shoulders. She was strong. She worked hard, she was smart, she was dedicated.

He was all of those things, too. But that didn't make them right for each other.

After an hour paddling into the wind, they slid their kayaks onto a short stretch of beach and climbed out, sitting in the wet sand. Jess leaned back against her elbows. "This couldn't be any more perfect. What a day."

O'Malley gazed out at the sparkling water. "Pretty nice," he agreed.

She dug in her daypack and handed him a plastic bottle of water, then settled back into the sand with her own. She unscrewed the top, her eyes still on the view as she took a long drink, letting water drip down her chin and onto her T-shirt.

"Jess—hell, are you doing your best to torture me?"

She grinned at him. "This isn't my best. I can do a lot better."

"Try me."

Her eyes widened—she hadn't expected him to throw down the gauntlet—but she sat up straight. "Ah. A challenge. I'm an attorney, O'Malley. I love a good challenge."

He swallowed some of his own water. "You're stalling, buying yourself time while you try to think of something."

He'd barely finished his sentence when she was on

top of him, straddling his lap, draping her arms over his shoulders, eye to eye with him. "There," she said. "I've thought of something. But we're exposed here. There's not much we can do without embarrassing ourselves."

"Kiss?"

"We could do that." She was a little breathless, and not just from kayaking. "But it might be worse than looking at wet spots on my T-shirt."

O'Malley decided not to let her off the hook. "Okay. Up to you. You're the one who loves a good challenge."

"You're just going to sit there, eh?"

"That's right."

She shifted on his lap. A provocative move. She leaned toward him and kissed him lightly on the mouth, then pulled back. He thought that would be it, which was a definite problem, but it wasn't. She kissed his nose, his forehead, then each cheek, until she found his mouth again, and this time, it was anything but a light kiss. He was trying to keep his hands off her, determinedly mashing them in the sand, just to amp up her sense of challenge, but it wasn't easy. His muscles were straining, his body responding to the play of her mouth on his, the touch of her fingers on his neck, in his hair.

Jess...

He didn't even know if he'd said her name out loud.

She broke off their kiss and tilted back from him. Her legs, he realized, were wrapped around his waist to anchor herself. "Oh, my." She took an exaggerated breath. "Wow. I did okay with that kiss, didn't I?"

"Jess—"

"I sort of like being bold like that. So much for the repressed New Englander."

O'Malley managed to clear his throat. "Jess—"

"I wonder if any fishermen saw us."

At that, he grabbed her by the hips, lifted her off him and sat her on the ground. He stood up and shook off the sand, resisting the temptation to howl at the ocean. Damn!

She smiled knowingly. "What, did you strain a muscle or something?"

"You're going to want to get your butt back in your kayak, because I'm not as puritanical as you are about who might see us making love on the beach."

"We could get arrested for public something-or-other." But she was scrambling for her kayak, grabbing her water bottle and dry pack. "You wouldn't want to get arrested in a foreign country."

He had her. She thought he'd do it. And it wasn't that he wouldn't take no for an answer. He would. But Jess wasn't so sure she could say no, that she wouldn't just take her chances and make love to him right there on a Canadian beach. For all they knew, a housing development was just over the knoll, or a group of bird-watching retirees was on its way there.

"You don't trust yourself to exercise good judgment in my presence," he said, amused.

She bent down to pick up her paddle, looking up at him, the sunlight catching those emerald eyes of hers. "You probably think making love on a beach is good judgment."

"Depends on the beach." He glanced around at the wet, fine sand, the protected horseshoe-shaped beach, the rise of sand and squat, gnarled evergreens that offered something of a screen to onlookers. Not that a passing boat wouldn't see everything. If the passengers were looking, of course. He shrugged. "This one seems fine."

But she wasn't taking any chances—with his power of persuasion or what the kiss had obviously done to her. She eased the kayak into the water and climbed in, shoving off with her paddle. "Coming?" she asked, looking back at him.

He grinned.

Then he wondered what her parents would do if he asked her to marry him. It popped into his mind as a joke, but it was like being sucker-punched.

Marry her.

His brother Mike had teased him on just that point for the past year, long before Brendan had ended up in bed with his dark-eyed prosecutor. He'd known Jess forever, it seemed. She'd always been there, frank, honest, idealistic, determined. Mike insisted she'd been half in love with Brendan for years.

"Fresh scallops," she said, as if she were snapping him out of a trance. "Iced tea. Fries. Coleslaw. Home-made pie. There has to be a place around here that serves homemade pie."

"Scallops aren't even a close second to sex."

She pretended not to hear him. Laughing, O'Malley shoved his kayak into the water and climbed in. Jess started paddling in steady, even strokes, and he noticed that her color was better. She didn't look as stressed out and overworked.

Must have been the bullet, him thinking about marrying her.

What he didn't want to do—never mind that Mike had vowed to flog him if he did—was to break Jess's heart.

CHAPTER
❧ FOUR ❧

S ummers had gone somewhere, but now they had to wait for Pat to finish up in his room.

Jess had fresh doubts about the wisdom of what she and O'Malley were doing, but, on the other hand, she trusted his instincts—and her own. Something was up with their fellow guest and their spooked hostess. Jess didn't have the urgent negative reaction to Summers that O'Malley did, but she definitely had the feeling he wasn't telling the entire truth about his stay at the Wild Raspberry.

Marianne needed more to take to the police than a throw that was out of place and the suspicion that someone was snooping on her. She wouldn't want to tarnish the image of her B and B, or offend her guests by overreacting to an incident—even several incidents—that could have innocent explanatons.

And focusing on Summers was easier than trying to figure out what she was going to do about Brendan O'Malley, Jess thought as she lingered in the second-floor hall.

He was right about her. She was falling for him.

She'd fallen for him a long time ago.

Refusing to admit she was in love with him was just a way of protecting herself. She didn't want to lose him as a friend. The thought of it made her sick to her stomach. He'd been a part of her life for ten years—why blow it now by telling him she was in love with him?

"Look at you," she whispered, "you're not even sweating."

He winked in that deliberately sexy way he had. "I'd have made a good criminal, don't you think?"

"Scary thought."

"Come on, you're a lawyer *and* an ex-cop. You've got nerves of steel."

She was surprised at how guilt-free and certain she

was about what they intended to do. "If Marianne catches us, she'll probably throw us out."

O'Malley was unperturbed. "Then we take the ferry back to Maine together. Preferably the overnight ferry. Make a real night of it."

"O'Malley, do you ever think about anything except how to get me back into bed?"

"You bet. What to do when I've got you there." He pressed a finger to his lips and lowered his voice even more. "Here she comes."

They ducked to one side of a glass-fronted bookcase in the hall as Pat, a woman around Marianne's age, lumbered down the steep stairs with a lightweight vacuum cleaner and a canvas bag of cleaning supplies slung over her shoulder. She was high energy and good-humored—and obviously hard-working. Having already cleaned the second-floor rooms, she continued on down to the first floor without noticing Jess and O'Malley.

"I can go up by myself," O'Malley said. "You can stay down here and be the lookout."

Jess shook her head. "I'm not going to let you do this by yourself."

"Sweetheart, if I go down, you go down. You

know the law. The guy driving the getaway car is just as culpable—"

"Quit arguing," she whispered, "and go."

Nothing about their escapade seemed to faze him. O'Malley was, without a doubt, Jess realized, a man who trusted his own judgment. He wasn't second-guessing himself now about his actions during the shooting because, fundamentally, he didn't question his instincts or his decisions that day.

So what about their night together? He was second-guessing himself all over the place about *that*.

He led the way up the stairs, which, unlike the stairs to the second floor, were carpeted. When they reached Summers's room, entry was no problem. O'Malley had "borrowed" the master key. If caught, he planned to explain himself to Marianne and ask for her indulgence. She'd probably let him off. Jess remembered Mike O'Malley telling her that his little brother Brendan had always been able to sweet-talk himself out of a tight spot.

Within thirty seconds, they were in Summers's room.

It smelled of cleaning products, and the streaks from the vacuum were still visible on the rug. The decor was quirky country cottage, but the colors were a bit more subdued than in her own room. The view of ocean and endless horizon through the floor-to-ceiling window needed no competition.

O'Malley immediately set to work, opening up the closet and rifling through their fellow guest's clothes. Keeping one eye on the door, Jess quickly checked the desk. She noticed a slim laptop computer, a stack of books on the history of Nova Scotia and a novel by an author named Alexander Crane.

"Well," Jess said, "nothing sensational in his reading habits."

"Hiking books?" O'Malley asked from the closet.

"Histories of Nova Scotia. Some of them look fairly old."

She opened the desk's center drawer and discovered a small basket of letters. Old letters, bundled together and tied with a grosgrain ribbon. Jess gingerly checked one of the dates.

August 1902.

"I think we're barking up the wrong tree, O'Malley."

He joined her at the desk. "Best we can do for loot is a stack of hundred-year-old letters?"

"They're not what you'd expect an avid hiker to have in his room," Jess said. "But this is an historic area. Maybe he's just interested in Nova Scotia's past."

O'Malley picked up the novel. "Even his reading material looks boring as hell."

"Alexander Crane—I've heard of him. He's a Canadian author. He's better known here than in the U.S., but he had a book a couple of years ago that was some kind of international bestseller. Remember?"

"No. Did you read it?"

Jess shook her head. "My mother's book club read it. They all liked it. He fictionalized some obscure but compelling Canadian historical event. I can't remember what it was."

"I guess it wasn't that compelling."

"No, it *was*." She tried to think. "I seem to remember it had a seafaring theme. It might have been about a Canadian ship that sank in the war. Something like that."

O'Malley frowned. "A ship sinking? You think that was it?"

"I'm not sure, but I know it had to do with the ocean. It might have been set on the west coast, though. I seem to remember something about Vancouver."

"Marianne told me something last night—" O'Malley

broke off and flipped the book over, staring at the black-and-white photograph of the author. "I'll be damned. Look at this, Stewart. It's our guy."

"Summers?"

"Alexander Crane. Maybe it's a pseudonym and John Summers is his real name, but they're the same guy."

Jess looked at the photograph, and the resemblance was there, unmistakable if not striking. The man staying with them at the Wild Raspberry was the same man identified as Alexander Crane in the photograph on the back cover of his book.

O'Malley tapped the photo with one finger. "He's grown a beard, his hair's grayer and he's lost weight and dropped the pipe-and-tweed look for the middle-aged hiker——"

"But it's the same man," Jess said. "Why would he come here in disguise?"

"So he could research a tragedy and look for sunken treasure without drawing attention to himself."

Jess nodded. "It makes sense."

Leaving the room the way they found it, they took the Alexander Crane novel with them and headed back downstairs.

Marianne was setting out tea on the back porch,

working quietly, obviously preoccupied. Jess hated having to tell her that one of her guests was, at best, staying there incognito. At worst, he was deliberately exploiting her and her friends for one of his books.

"Do you have a minute?" O'Malley asked softly.

Marianne didn't respond at first, then nodded, motioning to the wicker furniture. "Sit down, please."

Jess and O'Malley took side-by-side wicker chairs while Marianne sat on the very edge of a settee, her knees together, hands clasped in her lap as if she knew they were going to tell her something she didn't want to hear.

"How much do you know about John Summers?" Jess asked.

"Not much. He's been a good guest. Quiet. Friendly. Very intelligent."

O'Malley adopted the sensitive cop demeanor he used with traumatized witnesses. It was genuine, but he was also a professional. "How does he pay you?"

"Cash."

Jess said nothing, and neither did O'Malley as Marianne regarded both of them with fear and a measure of suspicion. "What is it?" she asked. "What's wrong?"

"Maybe nothing bad," O'Malley said. "We shouldn't jump to conclusions."

"He's not a friend of my ex-husband's. I'd know—" She took a shallow breath. "He'd never send a surrogate."

"Summers isn't who he says he is." O'Malley gave her the news about her guest in a straightforward manner, his tone gentle but not emotional.

"We're fairly certain that his real name is Alexander Crane," Jess added.

Marianne's eyes widened, not with fear or annoyance, but with tremendous relief and excitement, as if she were more than a little thrilled at the news. "Alexander Crane? You're kidding. Why, when John arrived here, my friends and I talked about how much he looks like Crane. We thought it was a coincidence. None of us looked into it. I mean, Alexander Crane is so well-known, and it just didn't occur to us—" She stopped a moment. "I never thought he'd lie about his identity."

"John, or Alexander Crane?" Jess asked.

Marianne understood what she meant. "I only know Crane by reputation. John—" Color rose in her cheeks, and she sat back, a touch of annoyance settling in. "Why would he lie? I don't understand. I would treat him like any other guest. I wouldn't care if he was a famous anything. He must know that by now, if he didn't at first."

O'Malley handed her the book, so that she could see the photo for herself. "Is Alexander Crane a pseudonym?" he asked.

"Not that I know of. No, I'm sure it's not."

"You never checked Crane's picture when you and your friends realized he resembled your guest?"

"No, of course not. I never for a second thought he and John really were one in the same, just that John resembled Alexander Crane." She rubbed the picture with two fingertips, as if she had to make sure it was real. Tears rose in her eyes. "I never—" She inhaled sharply. "Trust is a big issue with me. I don't like being lied to."

"He might have had valid reasons," Jess said quietly.

O'Malley shrugged. "I guess it's better to find a famous writer is hanging out in your attic than a bank robber."

"Or your abusive ex-husband," Marianne mumbled. "How could he let me think—"

She didn't finish, stumbling to her feet, shaken and upset, just as John Summers—aka Alexander

Crane—walked out onto the porch. "Liar," she whispered, crying, and pushed past him.

He went white and glared at Jess and O'Malley.

But the glare didn't last. His shoulders sagged, and he shook his head, sighing. "I knew you were on to me. Did you search my room? I honestly don't blame you. I don't know why I just didn't tell you the truth. Or Marianne."

"Why the false identity?" O'Malley asked.

"Privacy. I'm researching a new book. It's a sensitive subject in this area. I thought it best…" He sank into a chair, looking miserable amidst the cheerful surroundings. "It seemed like a good idea at the time."

Jess could feel the guy's agony. "But you didn't expect to fall for Marianne."

He didn't raise his head. "Given her background, I don't see how she's going to understand."

"Don't sell her short, Mr. Crane," Jess said. "It could depend on your reasons."

O'Malley was obviously not that interested in the romantic undertones of what was going on. "What about the snooping?"

Crane raised his head, frowning. "What snooping? I've conducted all my research off the premises.

Marianne... I suspect she has information I could use, but I was waiting for the right moment to tell her who I am and ask her indulgence. No, not waiting," he amended. "Postponing. I didn't want to face her sense of betrayal."

"You two have spent a lot of time together over the past month," Jess said. "You must have told her something about yourself."

"The surface stuff was all lies, but my thoughts and feelings—what matters most to me—" He broke off, exhaling loudly. "Damn it. I've blown it completely."

"Maybe you should talk to her," Jess suggested.

O'Malley got up, his cop radar obviously still pinging madly. "She thinks someone's gone through an old trunk of hers."

"That wasn't me! My God—you mean she thinks I've been sneaking around her house? I had no idea anything of the sort was going on. I knew she was upset about something, but it never occurred to me—" He seemed genuinely distraught. "I wish she'd told me about the snooping. I'd have told her the truth about me immediately."

"Then you didn't step over the line to research your book?" O'Malley asked.

"No. Absolutely not."

"What's it about?"

"I'd rather not say."

"You don't have to. I have a pretty good idea. An heiress and her Irish sailor boyfriend drowned just beyond the cove. Local legend says she had jewels and gold coins—"

"I'm not interested in treasure," Crane protested.

"Maybe not, but you're interested in their story. If Marianne decides to go to the police—"

"The police? For what? Operating under a false identity for research purposes may be a question of trust, but it's not that serious." He stopped, glancing from O'Malley to Jess and back again. "Tell me more about Marianne's suspicions."

"The contents of the trunk in the living room are from the early twentieth century," O'Malley told him. "Marianne's great-grandparents lived in this area. She says someone's been into the trunk." He regarded Crane a moment, then went on. "The letters in your room are from that same era."

"But I—" The writer seemed truly repentant, but also very unwilling to discuss his work. "I was waiting to ask her for information on her family's past. Her great-grandmother and Pat's great-grandmother were best friends when the *Osprey*—that's the name of the ill-fated boat with the supposed treasure—went down. Pat's great-grandmother lived here, in this house. Marianne's great-grandmother lived in the village."

Jess thought she could put the pieces together now. "So that's why you picked the Wild Raspberry. It wasn't just because it was in the area and had a room. It's because the women who own and operate it are descendants of characters in your book."

"It's not a book yet," he said, his voice barely audible. "So far it's just notes. The story's a mix of fact, fiction, myth and speculation. I'm not convinced the so-called treasure ever existed. I just wanted to get a feel for the area, the land, the air, the people."

"The treasure exists," Marianne said from the doorway, calmer now.

Crane surged to his feet, his anguish obvious. "Marianne, I'm sorry I didn't tell you the truth sooner—"

"You haven't told me the truth yet, Mr. Crane. I only know it from Mr. O'Malley and Ms. Stewart."

"I wanted to tell you. I must have started to a

hundred times, but I knew that once I told you, I'd have to leave. And I didn't want to."

"Because of your book," she said stiffly.

"No. I'll burn every word I've written tonight if it'll help restore your trust in me."

O'Malley cleared his throat. "So about this treasure…"

Marianne smiled at him. "It's buried in the back-yard."

Crane was stunned. "What?"

O'Malley turned to Jess and grinned. "I've never done buried treasure, have you?"

She hadn't.

"After I realized someone had been snooping around," Marianne went on, "I got out one of my great-grandmother's diaries and started reading it. There's a passage about the *Osprey*. Several passages, actually." She paused, pouring tea into a Beatrix Potter mug and staring at it, as if somehow it could help her to explain. "She and her friend Yvonne, Pat's great-grandmother, found the jewels and coins and buried them."

"Why?" O'Malley asked.

Crane didn't say a word. He was listening with intense interest, even fascination, as if all his research was making sense now as Marianne spoke about two long-dead friends.

"I think it was fear and a sense of romance that made them do what they did," she surmised. "They were ordinary women—they weren't heiresses. They were afraid they'd be accused of stealing or, worse, of having caused the *Osprey* to sink."

Jess tried to imagine two teenage girls from that era coping with such a tragedy so close to home. "And the romance? Where did that come in?"

"They didn't believe anyone should profit from such a tragedy," Marianne said with a touch of pride. "And they didn't want to give the jewels and coins back to the family. They blamed the family for what happened."

Crane shifted in his chair, some of his guilt and misery lifting. "The family was dead-set against the marriage, and not just the woman's parents. Her uncles and aunts, her grandparents, her older brothers and sisters—they all ganged up on her."

"So the girlfriends here in the sticks didn't want them getting back the loot," O'Malley said, and Jess knew he was trying to cut through some of the emotion in the room.

Marianne nodded. "If they'd tried to sell any of it themselves and were caught, they'd be rightly accused of stealing. It washed up on shore across the street from here, near the tide pool where you and I talked last night."

"Fate," Jess said. "What an amazing story."

O'Malley wasn't finished with it. "You said the treasure's buried in the backyard. Does that mean you know where?"

"It means I dug it up." Her eyes sparkled, and she let out a breath. "I can't tell you how relieved I am that my ex-husband hadn't somehow figured out that I might have buried treasure on the premises. I dug it up last night to check it was still there and reburied it immediately. It's under an old-fashioned pink rosebush that Pat's great-grandmother and my great-grandmother planted together to mark the spot. They're both still there—the rosebush and the treasure."

"Your friend Pat," Jess said. "Does she know?"

"No, I don't think so. I haven't said anything to her." Marianne dropped onto a chair, almost spilling her tea. "Oh. Oh, dear. Pat. She must have known our great-grandmothers' secret."

Jess exchanged a glance with O'Malley. "Pat cleans Mr. Crane's room," she said. "She could have figured out why he was here and been afraid he'd accuse your great-grandmothers of stealing the treasure."

"Poor Pat!" Marianne sighed. "She must have guessed there was something in the old photo albums and diaries in my trunk."

"Any indication she got to the rosebush before you did?" O'Malley asked.

Marianne shook her head. "I'm sure she just wanted to make certain there was nothing incriminating in the trunk. She must have been reading bits and pieces of the diaries at a time, when she could get to it. I have to find her and reassure her. I want her to read the diaries! There's so much about both our great-grandmothers in it. It's inspiring."

Crane got to his feet, his earlier melancholy gone. He cleared his throat. "Marianne, if you'll allow me, I'd like to join you—as a friend—when you talk to Pat. The book I'm writing—" He smiled tenderly at her. "There'll be other books."

"Mr. Crane—"

"Alex."

She smiled then, her earlier tension and fear

having disappeared, and set her tea down as she rose. "Thank you. I'm sure together we can convince her she has nothing to fear."

After Marianne and Crane headed out, O'Malley got up and dumped his tea over the porch rail into the grass. "What do you think was in it?"

"Tea leaves," Jess said.

"Nah. Something else. Tasted like someone put out a cigarette in it."

"It's Earl Grey tea, O'Malley."

He grinned at her. "I knew that."

"I know you did," she said. "You're just being obtuse on purpose."

"Had to break the spell before you got teary-eyed."

"Think Crane and Marianne are—"

"They're destined for each other," he said, finishing her thought. "It's like the muses drove the two of us here just to bring them together."

"Maybe so," Jess said. "What about us?"

"We didn't need the muses to drive us together, Stewart. We needed them to give us a swift kick."

"O'Malley—"

"I've been in love with you a long time, Jess. A long time."

"Me, too…with you. I just——" She quickly picked up the tea dishes, not knowing what else to do with herself. "I'm used to having you in my life, you know. As a friend."

"You're doing a pretty good job of getting used to me in your life as a lover."

She felt a rush of heat, then laughed. "I am, huh?"

He grinned at her. "I'd say so."

"I've been afraid of losing you altogether if the lover part didn't work out."

"I know."

"But friend *and* lover. That's the best of both worlds. I like that a lot. What about you?"

"Jess——damn. You've been in my life for ten years. I want you there for a hundred years. Hell, I want us to be together forever."

She believed him—he'd never been anything but straight with her. "What about the hockey sticks and the weights rolling around on the floor? And the way you've been living your life?"

"Ask the same questions about yourself."

She couldn't hold on to the tea dishes anymore and set them back on the table. "I'd say that I'm ready to make changes."

"So am I." He slipped his arms around her and kissed her, lingering close to her mouth, smiling. "I enjoy the hell out of kissing you."

"Your brothers—"

"Will be ecstatic. They like you. They think a lawyer in the family's just what we need. We've got everything else covered."

She smiled, feeling safe and warm and more content than she could ever remember. "They've been teaching me hockey on the sly so I'd know what to do with you."

He winked. "You know what to do with me."

"I have a mean slapshot."

"I can do a wicked body check."

She suddenly caught her breath. "I wonder how long Marianne and Crane will be gone."

"Not long enough." O'Malley pointed to the window, where their hostess, the author and Pat were making their way into the backyard. "The muses are having their fun with us now. It'd be rude to carry you upstairs when there's buried treasure to be dug up."

They decided to join Marianne, Pat and Alex Crane out at the rosebush. As she pulled herself together, Jess noticed the Shelternet sign again.

The courage to click.

Marianne Wells's new life—with all its challenges and rewards—had started with that first positive step of going to www.sheleternet.ca and finding the help she deserved.

She was an inspiration, Jess thought. No question about it. Last night, after the blueberry wine, Marianne had shown her and O'Malley the Sheleternet Web site. It had put Marianne in touch with a local shelter, just as it did thousands of women all across Canada. The site combined compassion and technology and provided a safe, anonymous environment for women to take those first scary, tentative steps into living a violence-free life.

As in the U.S., the Canadian statistics on domestic abuse were shocking. Each year, more than a hundred thousand Canadian children witnessed the abuse of their mothers. Worldwide, violence caused more deaths and ill health of women between the ages of fifteen and forty-four than malaria, traffic accidents and cancer combined.

Jess, who prosecuted such cases, welcomed the reminder of the positive message that Sheleternet offered to abused women and their children.

The courage to click.

It was a beginning.

"Jess?"

She realized she'd been lost in thought and smiled at O'Malley. He was a strong, intense man in a sometimes violent profession, and he loved to banter and tease and play hard—but he respected her.

And he loved her.

"I'm fine," she said. "More than fine."

He smiled. "Me, too."

Dear Reader,

In writing "Close Call" and getting to know the inspiring work of Jan Richardson and Kathryn Babcock with Shelternet, I was struck by the importance of something as simple as reaching out to others. Reaching out to help—and reaching out *for* help.

Shelternet provides abused women throughout Canada with a place where they can reach out anonymously, safely, for help. At Shelternet, they can find the location of the nearest shelter, information on how to form a safety plan, links to help lines and stories of other women who left abusive relationships. Shelternet also provides children and teens who've witnessed the abuse of their mothers with resources designed just for them.

To reach out to women in crisis, we have only to act on our intention and desire to help, whether it's with our time and effort or with a financial donation. I had the privilege of meeting Jan and Kathryn in person in Vancouver at the first More Than Words event. It was attended by 200 readers on a lovely evening, in a gorgeous setting, with all of us grateful that Shelternet is there when a woman reaches out for help. And I've no doubt I wasn't alone in coming away determined to do more myself to reach out to help.

For more information, please visit shelternet.ca today.

Thank you,

Carla Neggers

DENA WORTZEL

M *ore Than Words* could very well describe
Dena Wortzel's beliefs about books and
literacy. For Dena, books truly are more
than the words on the page—they're a way for us
to learn about ourselves, and to help us develop
passion and empathy. Reading has a healing quality
that can transform lives and, most important for
Dena, can transform families.

Ninety million adults in the United States have
limited literacy skills. Many of them are parents.
Motheread/Fatheread® is a literacy program that
focuses on *family* literacy. Established in 1987 in North
Carolina by Nancye Gaj, Motheread/Fatheread® has
gained national recognition for its innovation and ef-
fectiveness. Its emphasis on literacy in the context of

people's lives inspired Dena to spearhead the program in Wisconsin through the nonprofit Wisconsin Humanities Council. Motheread/Fatheread® helps parents improve their own literacy skills—and strengthen their family communication and relationships. Parents are helped to do the one thing that's been proven to lead to children's success in school: read with them daily.

Dena's own mother read to her daily. And as soon as Dena learned to read books herself, she read *constantly*. Dena describes herself as having been "a bookish child." She was always sitting in a corner reading, and she'd take a duffel bag full of books on family trips. Books were definitely part of her life growing up, part of *her*. And they still are.

Dena has always been strongly committed to helping people in need—to helping the poor and the powerless change their lives. She was involved in international development in third world countries, working in Sri Lanka before moving back to Wisconsin and joining the Wisconsin Humanities Council. Dena is deeply concerned with issues of social justice and people living in lesser circumstances—*and* she has this love of literature. It all comes together in Motheread/Fatheread®.

Dena doesn't divide the world into readers and nonreaders. She says it's all about what we've been exposed to. One of the main ways we understand our world is through storytelling, and books are one way to access stories. People who did not grow up reading latch on to reading when the stories and the books are meaningful to their lives. And as Dena points out, the reading material in Motheread/Fatheread® reflects what matters most in *all* our lives...our family relationships.

Motheread/Fatheread® doesn't address literacy as a skills deficit—and this is important to Dena. She emphasizes to parents in the program that they are caregivers of children and are there out of concern and love for their kids. They'd like their children to have a better time in school than they might have had.

The act of reading together is important in itself. Dena says, "It's a way for parents and children to spend time together and communicate about things that matter—rather than daily interactions like eat your peas. In this reading time parents and children are actually asking each other questions about what they think and feel. Parents are listening to their children." Many parents didn't know how to read to their kids because *they* were never read to as kids. Now they can sit with their children and read to them—even initiate play around the reading of books. Children and parents both benefit.

Before her recent promotion to executive director of the Wisconsin Humanities Council, Dena taught inmates in the Wisconsin correctional system using the materials of Motheread/Fatheread®. But Dena says she learned as much from the participants as they learned from her. "It's an extraordinary experience to meet with a group of adults, and within an hour or two of meeting, develop meaningful relationships, have meaningful conversations—connecting across vast distances of experience and speaking from the heart. They understand one another, share concern for one another—and their children—through books. It's miraculous. Simple, yet miraculous. And it is the power of stories that has brought on this miracle. Books are the entryway." By talking about characters and stories, the participants are identifying with the material, and identifying with each other. "Without books," Dena says, "they just wouldn't be having these conversations, these connections."

At the Wisconsin Humanities Council, Dena guides

her organization's collaborations with social service workers, librarians, teachers and others throughout the state who want to use this nationally recognized program to help families in their communities. Dena organizes the training of at least forty people a year to teach the Motheread/Fatheread® program—and those forty instructors can reach at least 800 families throughout Wisconsin annually. Many of the professionals Dena trains are swept up with the same enthusiasm she has for Motheread/Fatheread®, often saying it is the most exciting educational experience in their careers. One instructor was teaching a group of new immigrants using an African folktale about a village threatened by monsters. This opened up a discussion of what "monsters" have come into their lives—and the participants shared incredible stories of personal tragedy and strength.

Dena's desire to help those in need also extends to animals. She lives on a horse farm where her late husband specialized in rehabilitating horses with behavioral problems that others had given up on. Their efforts saved the lives of horses that might otherwise have been destroyed.

Dena really feels grateful about being in the world

and helping others—that she has been able to use her education and experience to better people's lives. Motheread/Fatheread® brings together two of Dena's passions—her love of literature and her desire to help those in need—in a way that inspires students and colleagues. Now Dena and her work with Motheread/Fatheread have become an inspiration for this book...and for others to reach out with the healing power of words.

For more information visit:
www.wisconsinhumanities.org/read/index.html
or write to Motheread/Fatheread®, c/o Wisconsin Humanities Council, 222 S. Bedford St., Suite F, Madison, WI 53703-3688.

SUSAN MALLERY
~∾— BUILT TO LAST —∾~

✢—SUSAN MALLERY—✢

Susan Mallery is a *New York Times* bestselling author of more than ninety romances. Her combination of humor, emotion and just-plain-sexy has made her a reader favorite. Susan makes her home in the Pacific Northwest with her handsome husband and possibly the world's cutest dog. Visit her Web site at www.SusanMallery.com .

CHAPTER
~ONE~

Marissa Spencer liked to think she preferred quiet, average men who were kind and funny, and that she never found herself attracted to brooding hunks. But in this case, she was willing to make an exception.

Aaron Cross had the body of a male centerfold, the face of an angel—fallen, of course—and dark eyes so filled with pain they could rip out her heart at fifty paces. Her friend Ruby would say that a man like Aaron was nothing but trouble, and in this case Marissa would have to agree. Still, she indulged herself in a look-fest while he completed his phone call.

She'd arrived a few minutes early for their 10:00 a.m. appointment. Based on what she'd heard about the amazingly talented and reclusive Mr. Cross, she'd expected a cranky old man. Sometimes surprise was a good thing, she thought when he hung up and turned to face her.

"Ms. Spencer," he said as he moved toward her, holding out his hand.

He was tall and she was a woman used to looking men in the eye. He wore his dark hair long and shaggy and walked with a grace that nearly took her breath away.

When she shook hands with him, she felt sparks that were so predictable, she nearly giggled. Of course, she thought, holding in a grin. With Joe, the sensible guy who ran the hardware store and kept asking her out, she felt nothing. But with danger-guy, she was all aquiver. So went her life.

"Marissa," she said when she could catch her breath to speak. "Thanks for seeing me."

He glanced at her, taking in the long wool skirt, cropped jacket and boots. It might be spring in the rest of the country, but here in Wisconsin, there was still snow on the ground.

"You said you had something unusual to discuss with me," he said, motioning to a leather chair in the corner of his showroom.

She'd already looked around and admired the amazing furniture he made. The hand-carved pieces were both strong and elegant. The fabrics he chose were distinctive, while much of the leather was reworked from older pieces.

As she sank into the seat, she wished her budget allowed for this kind of indulgence. But alas, her needs were more easily met at the local thrift store.

He perched on a stool, forcing her to look up to meet his gaze. As their eyes locked, she felt a definite shiver low in her belly. Was her attraction to this stranger really that intense, or was it just her second Danish of the morning talking back to her?

"I'm here to beg," Marissa said happily. "I could pretty it up for you, but that's the unvarnished truth. I'm on the acquisitions committee for a charity auction. We're raising money to buy books for our Motheread/Fatheread® program."

Aaron didn't blink as she spoke, which made it hard for her to judge his reaction.

"Are you horrified?" she asked.

"I'm listening."

She supposed that was something.

"I shouldn't really be here," she confessed with a grin. "While everyone agrees that your furniture is so amazing as to be brilliant, apparently you don't have a reputation as a joiner."

"I keep to myself," he admitted.

"That's what I heard. Everyone told me I was crazy to even ask, but hey, what's the worst that could happen? You say no. Which would be sad, because the program is amazing. We're teaching people to read—mostly parents."

She leaned forward and clasped her hands together. "You can't imagine how a person changes when he or she learns to read. There's such pride. Watching parents read a story to their children for the first time would totally break your heart. Reading gives them a chance to participate in their children's education—to be better parents. The purpose of the auction is to raise money to buy books."

The woman kept on talking. Her energy filled the

showroom until Aaron half expected to see mini bolts of lightning bounce off the ceiling and walls. Most of the locals knew enough to leave him alone, but not this one. She showed no signs of stopping.

"Who are you?" he asked, interrupting her in midsentence.

She frowned slightly. "I told you. Marissa Spencer."

"Not your name. Who you are. Why are you doing this?"

"Oh." She shimmied a little in her seat and smiled. "I moved here about two years ago. I'm a part-time bookkeeper, part-time librarian, and I volunteer a lot."

"So you think you can change the world?"

"Of course."

Figured. He knew the type. Those who still believed in happy endings and miracles.

"I don't think so," he said, standing.

She bounced to her feet. She was tall, blond. Pretty.

"If this isn't a good time, I can come back."

He saw it then, what he'd missed at first glance. Behind the long hair and the easy smile was a spine of steel.

"What can I say to make you go away?" he asked.

"Aside from a donation?"

He nodded.

"We could reschedule."

He was only a few years older than her, but he felt tired and worn by comparison.

"You're going to keep coming back, aren't you?"

She shrugged. "Sorry, but yes. I'm determined. It's a flaw."

She made the statement with a cheerfulness that told him she didn't consider it a flaw at all. Which meant the quickest way back to his solitude was to give her what she wanted and get her out of his life.

"What did you have in mind?" he asked.

Her blue eyes widened. "You mean you'll donate something?"

"Sure."

"Wow. That's great. Really. I don't know how to thank you."

"Pick something."

He motioned to the contents of the showroom. She walked to a small upright chair and ran her fingers over the carved wood.

He liked the way she took her time to study the piece. She noticed the little details and then stepped back to look at it from a distance. When she turned over the price tag, she went pale, and for a second he thought she was going to pass out.

"Okay, then," she said, straightening. "Maybe something smaller?"

He realized she had no idea who he was. To her he was a local recluse who made furniture. Not a man with a waiting list a year long and thousands of people willing to pay exorbitant prices for something made by him.

"I mean, it's all lovely, but we're talking a charity auction. We thought your piece would go for maybe five hundred dollars."

"I have some shavings out back," he said, holding in a smile.

She pretended to consider the possibility. "If we put them in containers, maybe. How about kindling from your workshop? I could sew up little bags and label them or something."

She was so earnest, he thought, amused for the first time in ages.

"I'll make a bookcase. It's not the sort of work I usually do, so there's no way to compare prices. It will be simple, but a good piece. How's that?"

Marissa clapped her hands together and spun in a circle. "That would be amazingly cool. I don't know what to say." She stopped the twirling and grinned at him. "You'll get a letter for tax purposes, of course."

"I thought I might."

"Maybe I'll bid on the bookcase myself."

He doubted that. She struck him as the type who never had two cents to rub together. No doubt she spent her spare time helping in a soup kitchen or working with sick kids at a hospital.

"Tell me when you need it by," he said, ready to end the conversation.

She pulled a small notebook out of her purse and read off a date. "And then there's the picnic next Saturday."

His gaze narrowed. "What picnic?"

"The one where we thank all the donors. You'll have to come because you're the grand prize, so to speak. The last item to be auctioned. Everyone is very excited to meet you." She bit her lower lip. "I sort of said you would be there."

Events like that were his idea of pure torture. "I'm making the bookcase. Isn't that enough?"

She sighed. "You'd think it would be, wouldn't

you? But there will be a lot of families at the picnic. You know, people who have completed the program, along with those just starting. And lots of kids. You're a real inspiration to them."

He doubted that. "Does anyone ever tell you no?"

"Oh, sure. Lots of times. At first anyway. It means I have to keep coming back and asking."

Which sounded a lot like a threat to him.

He wanted to swear. He wanted to complain he didn't have time and, more important, didn't want to make time. He wanted to tell her to get out of his life and never come back.

She looked at him with her big blue eyes and trusting expression. As if she believed down to her bones that there was nothing in the world he wanted more than to go to her picnic. In the past he'd always found it easy to tell people no, but for some reason, right now he couldn't seem to speak the word.

"What time?" he asked.

Marissa beamed at him. "Eleven. You don't have to bring anything. We're providing the food. I'm making brownies and the Main Street deli is donating sandwiches. You'll have a great time. I can't wait."

"Yeah. Me, too."

Her gaze slipped past him to settle on something over his shoulder. She opened her mouth, then closed it.

He turned and saw Buddy standing in the doorway of the showroom.

The coyote still had much of his winter coat, making him seem bigger than usual. His dark eyes never left Marissa as he sniffed the air to catch her scent.

"A friend of yours?" she asked.

He liked the fact she didn't call Buddy a pet. "He hangs out around here. When he was young, he got caught in a trap. I rescued him. He healed, but he's got a bum leg and can't survive on his own."

"Is he tame?"

"Sometimes."

She turned her attention from the coyote back to him. "Why do I suddenly think you're not as mean and tough as you want the world to believe?"

"Think what you want."

"I will." She smiled. "Thank you, Aaron. For the donation and for spending time with me. I look forward to seeing you at the picnic." She glanced again at Buddy, then left the showroom.

Aaron and Buddy watched her go. When they were alone, the coyote approached and Aaron rubbed his ears.

"What do you think?" he asked the silent creature. "Women like that are trouble."

Buddy sniffed and Aaron grinned. "You're right. She sure did smell good."

CHAPTER
~TWO~

"He's totally hot," Ruby said as she unpacked supplies for the picnic.

"Maybe, but that doesn't make him my type." As Marissa spoke, she was careful to keep her left hand—and her crossed fingers—out of sight. She didn't want to actually be *lying*.

"But he's wounded," Ruby said, her expression knowing. "You love that. Lord knows you can't seem to avoid a broken man. Show you someone normal, successful and interested in settling down, and you run screaming in the opposite direction. But if there's a battered soul within fifty miles, you're trembling with desire."

Marissa wrinkled her nose. "I do not tremble with desire."

"You do something, girlfriend, and it's not healthy."

Marissa knew better than to argue. Her track record with men bordered on pathetic. Unfortunately she *was* attracted to men with issues—men who tended to move on after solving their issues. Wasn't that just the way of it?

"Aaron's not like that," she said as she opened packages of paper plates. "He's very successful and normal."

Ruby snorted. "Sure. That's why he keeps to himself all the time. And what's up with that wolf of his?"

"I think Buddy's a coyote."

"Whatever. Can't the man get a lab or golden retriever like the rest of the world?"

"He rescued Buddy."

"Maybe. All I'm saying is you've been acting goofy ever since you met the guy. I can read the signs. You're already crazy about him, and from what I've heard, he's going to break your heart. Why don't you try staying safe for once?"

Good advice, Marissa thought as she watched her friend toss her long braids back over her shoulder and start setting out the wrapped sandwiches.

"I'm not crazy about him," Marissa said as she put out containers of fruit salad. "I think he's interesting."

"Uh-huh. You did five minutes on his butt two days ago. Before that it was his face, and then how beautiful his furniture is."

Marissa felt the heat of a blush on her cheeks. Had she really been that bad?

"His furniture *is* beautiful. You should go to his showroom sometime."

"And be a nice juicy replacement for coyote chow? No thanks. Besides, I don't have a spare twenty thousand for an original Aaron Cross table."

Marissa thought about the price tag on the simple chair she'd seen. "Yeah, he does make the big bucks."

Ruby grinned. "At least that's a change. Usually you go for guys who are dead broke. This time you won't be making his car payments."

Marissa put her hands on her hips. "That happened once, and you promised to never mention it again."

"You're right. Sorry. I just want to see you happy. With someone who'll treat you right."

That was exactly what Marissa wanted, too. She tried not to be envious of Ruby's great husband and her two kids, but sometimes it was tough. Why couldn't she find the same?

She had to admit her usually lousy taste in men complicated the issue. She did attract those in need of rescuing. Unfortunately she found it difficult to say no to anyone in need.

"So when does Mr. Tall, Dark and Weird arrive?" Ruby asked.

"He's not weird, and he didn't say what time he'd be here."

"Want to bet he's not going to show?"

"He'll be here," Marissa said with an assurance she didn't feel. As much as she wanted to believe Aaron would come, she was starting to have doubts. Somehow he didn't strike her as the picnic type.

Aaron sat in his truck a full five minutes after he'd parked. He could see the crowd of people gathered around the wooden table. To the left, kids chased a couple of soccer balls; to the right, someone had started a fire in one of the pits. Altogether too much life for his liking. He was about to put the truck in Reverse when he saw a tall blond woman pick up a toddler, swing the child around and laugh.

He recognized Marissa even as he refused to acknowledge the ache that seeing her had started. Yeah, she was attractive and he liked her smile, and maybe he appreciated that she still saw the best in people when he'd long since given up hope. But that didn't mean he wanted anything to do with her. Or her causes.

Still, he found himself opening the door and stepping out into the sunny April afternoon. Spring had arrived in Madison and everyone seemed to appreciate the fact. Sounds carried to him—the laughter and shrieks of children, the conversation of adults. In the distance, a couple of dogs barked. Still, for him, the world narrowed as Marissa glanced up. She held the child, but her attention was on him. Their gazes locked in a moment of pure connection.

The ache intensified. He walked toward her, telling himself he was a fool for bothering. He'd never thought to check for a wedding ring when she'd been in his shop. It figured that the only woman to catch his interest in the past five years might be married.

"You came," she said with a smile that lit up her

whole face. "Of course, I knew you would, but you hadn't exactly said so."

She was lying, he thought, and doing a piss-poor job of it. "I didn't know I was coming until I got here," he told her. He nodded at the kid. "Yours?"

"What? No. No husband, no kids. This is Tamara, my friend Ruby's daughter. Tamara, this is Mr. Cross."

The toddler buried her face in Marissa's shoulder.

"That age," Marissa said. "She's shy. Come on. I'll return this little sweetie to her mom, then introduce you around. Or do you know everyone?"

Aaron glanced at the crowd. He might have made his home here for the past five years, but he'd never been one to socialize.

"Can't say that I do."

"You will after today."

Marissa was as good as her word. He met everyone associated with the Motheread/Fatheread® program, along with town dignitaries, several local business owners and dozens of program graduates. People were lining up for sandwiches when a teenage girl rushed toward him.

"You're Aaron Cross," she shrieked, clutching a thick magazine to her chest. "Oh, I knew it! My friend

Heather called me so I found the magazine with your picture. Can you sign it for me?"

She thrust out a trendy magazine that had done a spread on his furniture a couple of months ago.

"I don't have a pen," Aaron said, wishing he'd never bothered to show up.

The girl handed him one as she danced from foot to foot. "I can't believe you're really here. Someone said you live in town. Is that true?"

"I, uh—"

"Jenny, why don't you let Mr. Cross get some lunch," Marissa said. "We don't want to scare him off, now do we?"

She gently led the teenager away, then urged Aaron into line for lunch. He glanced longingly toward his truck but knew he needed to wait until he wasn't the center of attention before bolting.

Even as he berated himself for showing up in the first place, he made conversation with the people in line. They were friendly enough, and none of them were holding magazines for him to sign. When he'd collected his food, he made his way to a dry spot a few yards from the picnic tables and settled against a tree. Marissa had been called away by one of the organizers, which meant if Aaron timed it right, he could be out of here in about fifteen minutes.

He bit into his sandwich, then reached down for his can of soda.

"Hi."

He turned toward the speaker. "Hi, yourself."

A young boy stood next to him. The kid was maybe six or seven, with tousled dark hair and a big red car on the front of his sweatshirt. He held a large picture book on cars in both hands.

"Whatcha got there?" Aaron asked when the boy didn't speak again.

"Is that your truck?" the boy asked, pointing to Aaron's large vehicle.

"Uh-huh. Do you like trucks?"

The boy nodded. He held up his book. "I like cars, too. They go fast."

"So I've heard."

Aaron felt torn. Part of him still wanted to escape to the solitude of his shop, but he wasn't willing to simply walk away from the kid.

"Is your mom here?" he asked.

The boy pointed to a group of adults laughing at one of the tables.

"I can read," the boy said. "Want me to read you this story?"

Aaron felt the weight of the inevitable drop onto his shoulders. He wrapped up his sandwich and moved it to one side before patting the ground next to him.

"Sure. What's your name?"

"Christopher."

The boy dropped to his knees and held the book out in front of him. It was already open to the first page.

"'Look at the cars,'" he said, reading slowly. "'Many, many cars. Some are red. Some are green. Some go fast.'" He glanced at Aaron, then pointed to the page. "That's the red one."

"I see that."

Aaron gave his truck one last, longing look before turning his attention to the boy. "What happens next?"

"I don't know what to say," Ruby admitted in a low voice.

Marissa shared her confusion. While she was delighted that Aaron had showed up at the picnic, she'd never expected him to stick around for very long. And if someone had asked her if he liked kids, she would have put her meager savings on a definite no!

But there he sat, under a tree, surrounded by at least six little kids. They all had new books they'd earned for their excellent reading skills and were taking turns reading aloud to him.

"The man has the patience of a saint or else he's touched in the head," Ruby told her.

"I don't think he's a saint," Marissa said, watching him laugh with a little girl as she pointed out a picture of a mouse dressed up like a princess. "I guess I should rescue him."

"Seems to me he's big enough to rescue himself."

Marissa wasn't so sure.

"At least he's not like the usual guys you get involved with," Ruby said. "That's something. I was doubtful, I'll admit it, but now I give him a big thumbs-up."

Marissa shook her head. "We're not dating."

Ruby smiled. "Maybe not, but you will be. Mark my words."

CHAPTER THREE

"**Y**ou didn't have to stay and help me clean up," Marissa said as she collected leftover sandwiches and put them into a basket. "No problem."

Aaron's low voice rumbled through the late afternoon and made her want to shiver. Not from cold, but from, well, him.

She knew she shouldn't keep looking at him, but she couldn't help darting quick glances every couple of seconds, as if to confirm he was still there, picking up empty soda cans and dropping them into the recycling bins.

"Besides, I owe you," he said with a smile. "You saved me."

She laughed. "I was afraid those kids were going to wear you out. All that reading."

"It wasn't so bad. Were they all part of the Motheread/Fatheread® program?"

"Their parents are."

"Those kids sure loved their books."

"It's fun to watch them pick out their first book. They treat the decision with such seriousness." She glanced up again and found him watching her. "What?"

"Just you." He jerked his chin toward the basket of leftover food. "Let me guess. You're taking it to a shelter."

"Of course. I couldn't just throw it out."

"Right. And these?" He pointed to the cans.

"We collect them all month, then take them in to the recycling center and use the money for an emergency fund."

"There's something wrong with you," he said.

"Because I care?"

"Because you care too much."

He stood there, lean and tall and ultramasculine. He might not approve of her, but she couldn't help approving of him. Strength radiated from him. His handsome, chiseled features made her want to trace the lines of his face. He looked like the kind of man who could withstand whatever life had to offer and still come out ahead.

He bent down to tie off the last of the trash bags, then leaned against a picnic table.

"Tell me, Marissa Spencer, have you ever done anything wrong in your entire life?" he asked.

She closed the basket and slipped on her sweater. "Silly question. Of course I have."

"Name it."

"I got into fights, brought a knife to school and set fire to the girls' locker room."

He frowned. "Not you."

"Yes, me." She slid onto the picnic table and put her feet on the bench seat. "I was nothing but trouble all the way through school."

"I don't believe you."

"Amazingly enough, that doesn't change what happened. Once I spent an entire summer locked up in juvenile detention."

She had the satisfaction of seeing the usually emotionless Aaron look shocked.

"But you're a goody-goody," he told her.

"Not exactly. I'm a person who wants to change the world. There's a difference."

"Explain it to me."

Marissa thought about her past. So much had changed for her that those troubled days seemed to belong to another lifetime.

"I used to frustrate my teachers because they knew I was smart enough to do the work, but I simply wouldn't bother. One day I'd done something—I can't remember what—and one of my teachers had had enough. She told me I had a choice. I could be suspended or I could work off my punishment in another way." She smiled. "There was this cute guy I liked, so I didn't want to get kicked out of school. I took Plan B."

"Which was?"

"Helping another student with his reading. I had to work with him every day after school. At first it was torture. I couldn't stand it. But after a while, I really started to like it." She smiled. "Then his reading improved, and I felt as if I'd just done something amazing. I offered to help someone else, and within a few weeks I realized that I could make a difference in a person's life. It was a liberating thought and it changed me completely."

"In what way?"

"I'd been bounced around in various foster homes from the time I was twelve. I didn't have a clue what I wanted to do with my life, I just wanted to be on my own. After the reading experience, I decided to go to college, where I majored in library science and sociology. I received my master's in social work and then settled here."

"Where you help everyone and volunteer in your free time."

"It's not like that," she told him. "I'm not perfect. I'm not a goody-goody, as you claimed. What I learned when I was sixteen was that I can make a difference. I can change someone's life for the better with only a little effort and time. Why wouldn't I want to do that? People ask me why I give so much. What I want to ask them is why they aren't getting involved."

He folded his arms over his chest. "Some people don't see the point."

Was he speaking about himself? "Maybe they haven't tried."

"Maybe they think no good deed goes unpunished."

"Ouch." She winced. "You don't actually believe that."

He shrugged. "There are a lot of things in this world we can't control."

"All the more reason to improve what we can."

"You're naive."

"You're a cynic."

He surprised her by smiling. "You left out grumpy."

She laughed. "Okay, a grumpy cynic. How can someone who doesn't believe in the world create such beauty? Your furniture gives pleasure to people."

"They also pay dearly for the privilege of owning it."

"So you're only in it for the money?"

"Sure."

She studied his dark eyes. "I don't believe you. I think you create such beautiful things because they matter to you."

"Believe what you want—it's the truth." His humor faded. "I'm not some project you can take on, Marissa. Don't try to save me."

"I wouldn't do that."

His gaze never left her face. "You're not a very good liar."

She hadn't actually planned on saving him, but maybe she had considered bringing him out of his self-imposed isolation.

"You shouldn't shut yourself away," she told him. "It's not healthy."

"Neither is running around worrying about everyone else so you don't have time to worry about yourself. Who looks after you?"

Interesting question. Even more intriguing, how had he figured her out so quickly?

"I can take care of myself," she said firmly.

"Something you've been doing since you were a kid."

"Exactly. I've had lots of practice and I'm good at it."

Pushing away from his table and walking toward hers, he moved closer. With every step he took, her breath hitched a little.

"Like I said, you're not a good liar."

She stared at him. "I'm telling the truth. I handle things just fine on my own."

"Uh-huh." He didn't sound convinced.

He stopped scant inches from her. He was close enough that she had to tilt her head to meet his dark gaze. Something flashed in his eyes, but she couldn't read it—probably because she couldn't think.

He put one hand on her shoulder. The heavy weight was warm and comforting, but also...exciting.

"Sometimes it's best to leave things as they are," he said, right before he lowered his head and kissed her.

Marissa had less than a second to brace herself for the impact of his mouth on hers. She wasn't sure what to expect, but it wasn't the light, tender brush of firm lips against her own.

He didn't claim her or push her, instead he gently kissed her, as if she were special and easily frightened. The hand on her shoulder moved to the back of her neck, where he rubbed her skin. His other hand cupped her chin.

Heat rushed through her, dousing her in need. Her stomach constricted, her chest got tight, and suddenly it was difficult to catch her breath.

When he stepped away, she had a feeling she looked as stunned as she felt.

"Why did you do that?" she asked.

He raised one eyebrow. "Hell if I know."

* * *

Aaron helped Marissa load her car with the left-over food and bagged aluminum cans. He waited until she was safely out of the parking lot before making his way home.

The sun had set by the time he pulled into the long road that led to his driveway. The automatic outside lights had already clicked on. After he parked he went into the house, but didn't bother turning on lamps. For some reason he wanted to stay in the darkness. As if hiding would help.

None of this should have happened, he thought as he set out food for Buddy, then grabbed a beer and walked into the family room. He sat in his favorite chair and stared out through the curtainless windows into the night. Not the day spent at the picnic or the kiss. He'd been telling Marissa the truth when he said he didn't know why he'd done it.

She wasn't what he'd expected, he admitted to himself. He would have guessed she'd been raised with money and a guilty conscience. Instead she'd learned her lessons the hard way. Her intelligence and humor appealed to him, and Lord knows, she was plenty easy on the eyes.

But not for him.

Darkness invaded his house. Even so, he turned his head toward the chest that sat tucked in the corner. He knew what lay inside. Talismans and memories. He'd been through the contents so many times, he knew them by heart.

Thinking about what had been, what he had lost, made him ache. If only…

Aaron drank down his beer, then set the bottle on a table. He closed his eyes and waited for the ghosts.

They came sometime before dawn. He'd retreated to bed around midnight and had tossed and turned for an hour. But now he slept, trapped by exhaustion. At first everything in the dream was fine. He saw Jilly as she'd looked when they'd first met. So young, he thought—had she really been that young? Barely eighteen and laughing. Always laughing. He saw her father's stern face—the old man had never approved of Aaron. No daughter of a colonel should be dating an enlisted man, even a Marine. But Jilly had stood firm against her father. She'd proclaimed her love for Aaron for all the world to hear. And the colonel had given in.

Next, he saw the wedding. The men in uniform, the toasts, the cake. He heard bits of conversation, the recitation of the vows and Jilly's laughter. Always her laughter.

Time moved forward again, to her knowing smile as she handed him the small, flat package containing a baby blanket. Deep in his sleep, he smiled as the feeling of elation rushed back to him.

He saw the ultrasound and the promise of their son. And then the orders came that sent him far away.

He'd been home for the happy birth, but had left again only a few weeks later.

The dream turned, shifted, got dark and cold. Pain swept through Aaron, immobilizing him. He knew what was coming, reached out to stop it, but he couldn't. Not then and certainly not now.

A rainy street. That dangerous time between day and night. Shadows. Too many shadows. He might have been half a world away, but he saw it as if he rode in the car with them. Jilly and little Matt. She was singing. He shouldn't have known that, but he felt it deep in his gut. She'd been singing as the drunk swerved through the stop sign and plowed into her small car.

Then the singing stopped.

Aaron came awake in a single breath. Sweat drenched his body and made him shiver, but he didn't reach for the covers. He heard the light clicking of Buddy walking toward him. Something had alerted the coyote. Had he cried out, or did Buddy simply sense his pain?

The ghosts turned to mist and faded. He watched them go, knowing he couldn't make them stay. When they were gone, it was as if he'd lost Jilly and Matt all over again.

Aaron didn't bother trying to go back to sleep. By five-thirty he was in his workshop. Buddy lay curled up on his bed in the corner, although he kept a watchful eye on Aaron.

"I'm all right," he told the coyote as he sipped coffee. "As all right as I'm going to get."

It had been six years since the car accident that had killed his wife and son. He'd left the Marines and had wandered around the country, looking for something he could never find. Eventually he'd settled here and started making furniture.

At first the ghosts had come every night. Eventually they'd haunted him weekly, then monthly. Now they rarely came. But he'd known they would be there last night.

What had called them? His time with those children? Or Marissa?

Did it matter? In the end, he only had to remember not to get involved. Caring, wanting, needing—they all led to pain. When he'd lost his family, he'd vowed never to love again. Keeping that promise had been a whole lot easier than he'd figured it would be.

CHAPTER
~ FOUR ~

Marissa stopped the car in front of the woodshop and drew in a deep breath. She couldn't seem to make the nerves in her stomach stop dancing. The weird tingling sensation that filled her whenever she thought about Aaron had only intensified since she'd driven onto his property. Telling herself she was here for a really good reason and not just because he'd kissed her didn't help.

"It didn't mean anything," she muttered under her breath. "It was just one of those things." Except she didn't know which thing.

"Did you say something, Marissa?" Tim Evans asked from the back seat.

"No. Just mumbling things. Old people do that from time to time."

Tom, Tim's twin brother, turned in his seat and patted her arm. "You're getting senile, aren't you? Should we be thinking about medication?"

"Very funny," she said with a grin. "Okay, you guys give me a second. I'm going to go talk to Mr. Cross."

Tim, the serious one of the two, met her gaze in the rearview mirror. "You didn't tell him we were coming, did you."

"Nope. But Mr. Cross loves surprises."

As she spoke, she carefully crossed her fingers, then she opened her door and stepped out into the warm Saturday morning.

The air smelled fresh and clean from the rain two days ago. Spring was showing off with new leaves and plenty of late daffodils and tulips. Marissa paused to admire the beauty of the rural setting, ignoring the voice in her head reminding her that putting off the inevitable wouldn't make it go away.

"Maybe Aaron really *does* like surprises," she whispered to herself as she made her way to his workshop and pushed open the door. And maybe next week Buddy would take to flying across the night sky.

"Hi," she yelled as she stepped inside the noisy room. "It's Marissa. Anybody home?"

She hadn't seen him since the picnic the previous weekend, and though she'd been thinking about him almost constantly, there was no excuse for the sudden thrill that shot through her at the sight of him now.

Aaron stood behind some woodworking tool that was nearly as tall as he. He wore goggles and something over his ears. Wood chips covered him, but somehow they only added to his charm.

He moved the equipment with a confidence that came from familiarity. A half-finished chair sat on the table next to him. From where she stood, she saw an open door leading to the woods behind the property. Buddy was lying in a patch of sun, watching her anxiously.

Aaron obviously hadn't heard her enter. He continued to work for several seconds before he looked up and she waved. When he clicked off the machine, a rush of silence filled the room.

"Hi," she said, hoping she sounded more cheerful

than anxious. "How's it going? Did you have a good week? Isn't the weather great?"

He pulled off his goggles and brushed back his dark hair. His gaze narrowed. "What's wrong?" he asked.

"Nothing. Why?"

"You're nervous. You've done something. What is it?"

"Me? No." She went for a smile, then sighed. "Okay. So, maybe. See, I brought Tim and Tom Evans with me. I thought they could spend the afternoon out here and you could show them what you do."

"No." He slid on his goggles and reached for the switch on the machine.

"Aaron, please."

He glared at her. "Marissa, you don't have the right to invade my life."

"I know. It's just…"

"I'm not interested in saving the world. That's your job."

They'd talked about that before. Was that why he hadn't called her to get together again? But he'd kissed her. Hadn't that meant anything? She nearly stomped her foot on the cement floor. Questions like that had haunted her for the past week. She should just come out and ask what had happened, except that would require a level of maturity she'd yet to master.

She drew courage from the fact that he hadn't restarted the machine.

"Their mother has cancer," she said quietly. "She's dying. It's just a matter of a couple of weeks or maybe even days. They're only fifteen, scared, and their dad is a wreck. Both sets of grandparents are hovering. I had to get them out of the house, but then I didn't know what to do with them. They need a distraction. Something physical."

Aaron silently ran through every swearword he knew.

"You don't play fair, do you?" he asked.

"This isn't a game. Not to them."

At the picnic she'd worn jeans and a long-sleeved T-shirt that had hugged her curves in a way designed to make a man go slowly mad. Today she'd dressed in another long skirt, with boots and a loose blouse. He'd spent the better part of a week doing his best *not* to think about her, which was pretty much the same as thinking about her all the time.

"Why me?" he asked.

"I didn't have anywhere else to go."

He knew what she wanted—to drag him into her "heal the world, one good deed at a time" philosophy. She wanted him to be a true believer, like her.

Well, that wasn't going to happen. He didn't need her or anyone else to get by.

The door to the shop opened slowly and two boys walked in.

"Marissa, is everything okay?" one of them asked.

They looked enough alike to be able to get away with murder, he thought. Young. All arms and legs, awkward, lanky. Scared.

Instead of answering the question, she looked at him. He felt her silent pleading. He should be furious with her for putting him on the spot like this, and he would be. Later.

"I'm Aaron Cross," he said as he tossed the goggles onto the table and walked toward the boys.

One of the twins moved toward him. "Hi. I'm Tom. That's Tim." Tom looked around. "You really make all your furniture here?"

"Every stick of it."

"That's so cool. What's that?" He pointed at a lathe. "What does it do?"

"Come on. I'll give you the grand tour." He turned to Tim. "Interested?" he asked.

The quieter twin nodded and moved closer. "Yes, Mr. Cross. Thanks for letting us stop by."

"Aaron," he said. "I'm not old enough to be Mr. Cross, yet."

Tom smiled. Tim still looked out of place. Aaron frowned as he realized the boys were identical, yet he knew exactly who was who. What was up with that?

"So what time should I come back?" Marissa asked. "I said I'd take the boys home around four, but I can come sooner and we can go to the mall or something."

Aaron glanced at the clock. It was barely after ten.

"Three-thirty is fine."

Marissa's eyes widened. "Are you sure?"

"Yeah." He glanced at the boys. "You two up for sandwiches for lunch? That's about all I have around here."

The twins glanced at each other and smiled. "That sounds good," Tom said. Tim nodded.

Marissa beamed. "Great. I'll see you guys later."

"You can't just show up like that," Aaron said two days later when Marissa dropped by with some banana bread as a thank-you for what he'd done for the twins.

"I know." She sat curled up in a corner chair in his workshop while he paced and looked fierce.

"It's not right. It's not fair to me or them."

"I'll agree that it's not fair to you," she said, hoping he wasn't as annoyed as he seemed. "But the boys were transformed. They talked about their day with you the whole way home. Besides, it can't have been that bad. You invited them back."

He turned to glare at her. "They're making some shelves for their room and they're not done. What was I supposed to do? Leave the project unfinished?"

"Of course not. That would have been horrible."

His gaze narrowed. "Are you making fun of me?"

"Me? Never. I'm simply pointing out that you had a good time, too."

He folded his arms over his chest. "That doesn't give you the right to do things like that."

She knew he had a point. "I'm sorry. It was sort of an emergency."

"You're the kind of person who always has emergencies. Don't involve me in the next one."

"Okay. I promise."

"Do you mean that?"

She nodded, careful to keep her crossed fingers out of sight.

"You look really cute when you're mad," she said.

"Marissa!"

Her name came out as a growl. The low, forceful sound made her all quivery inside. She wondered if he wanted to kiss her as much as she wanted him to.

"Do we have an understanding?" he asked.

"Sure. There's a spaghetti dinner at the Methodist church tonight. Usually those things are a bust because it's only five dollars and how good could the food be? But this is different. I know the lady who makes the sauce, and I have to tell you, it's fabulous. Plus there's garlic bread, and the money raised is for the new roof. Want to go?"

"No."

"Oh."

Suddenly she felt small and foolish. As if he really meant what he said. "Okay." She stood. "I need to get back to work. Thanks again for helping with Tim and Tom. You were terrific. I'll try not to bother you again."

She crossed to the door. Behind her, Aaron sighed.

"What time?"

She spun back to face him. "For dinner?"

He sighed again. "Yeah. What time should I pick you up?"

Her heart did a little happy dance and her insides did a shimmy. "Six-thirty."

Aaron was willing to accept the twins hanging around all the time, and the spaghetti dinner at the church, and the newspaper interview about his work in support of the auction. He didn't mind that he was asked to clean out his closets for the women's shelter rummage sale or the sixteen boxes of cookies he bought from the marching band kids who "just happened to stop by" with Marissa one afternoon. But when the vice principal of the local middle school wanted him to come in and talk on career day, he knew things had gone too far. Despite her promise to the contrary, Marissa was taking over his life and she had to be stopped.

He drove out one evening, intending to catch her before she started her Tuesday night Motheread/Fatheread® class.

"The woman is nuts," he muttered as he drove through the quiet streets toward the library. "Certifiably insane."

He could understand her need to change the world. Fine. That was *her* decision. He didn't want any part of it.

He was going to tell her that, along with a few other choice things. He had a mental list.

The library parking lot was nearly full. He found a spot near the back and headed inside toward the classrooms.

When he reached Marissa's, he stopped just outside the open door. The room was already filled with her students. He checked his watch and realized there were still fifteen minutes until the class officially began, but apparently these students didn't want to be late.

Nor did they stay in their seats. He glanced inside and saw several crowding around her desk. One middle-aged woman held up a single sheet of paper.

"From my Joe's teacher," she said proudly. "He is doing so good in his English class. She says it right here." The woman pointed to the paper. "I can read it, Miss Marissa. I can read it!"

Aaron knew there was a time to stand strong and a time for a strategic retreat. No way could he win tonight. Not here. Not like this. But soon he would find a way to get through to her and get her out of his life.

CHAPTER
~FIVE~

"Safety first," Aaron said. "No goggles, no class."

The half dozen teenagers crowded around his largest work- table nodded vigorously.

"Okay. See you next week," he told them.

"Thanks, Aaron," Tom Evans said as he and his brother headed for the exit. Two girls trailed after them, with the last couple of guys bringing up the rear.

Aaron waved, then dropped his own goggles to the bench and shook his head. How had this happened? He'd gone from helping grieving twins build a shelf to teaching an entire class. It was Marissa, he thought grimly. Somehow she'd sucked him into her world when he'd been so determined to stay out of it.

"You're looking serious about something," she said, stepping into the workshop.

Her unexpected appearance surprised him. Had he conjured her just by thinking about her? He wouldn't put it past her to figure out how to crawl into his brain.

"I wasn't expecting you," he said.

"I know. I was in the neighborhood."

He raised one eyebrow. "I'm the only one who lives on this road."

She smiled. "Maybe I got lost."

He doubted that. She always knew exactly where she was going. He eyed the foil-wrapped package she held.

"Okay, what is it?" he asked. "Somebody's having a baby and you want me to build the crib."

"Not at all."

"You need me to buy a printing press for the high school newspaper."

"Not even close." She tilted her head so her long blond hair tumbled over her shoulder. "What makes you think I want anything at all?"

"You're bringing me food. That's usually a sign. You bribe me with sugar."

"Not in this case."

Spring had arrived in full force, and with it came sunny days and warm temperatures. Marissa had traded in her long heavy skirts for shorter, softer ones that flirted with her knees and outlined her hips. Gone were the thick sweaters, and in their place were snug little T-shirts. If he were given the choice between whatever she'd brought on that foil-wrapped plate and the woman herself, there'd be no contest.

Still, he didn't move toward her or try to touch her. She might have found a way into his life, but he was careful to keep his emotions out of reach. He would admit to liking her, but nothing more. Nothing dangerous.

She set the plate on a worktable. "This is a freebee. Mostly me thanking you for everything."

Why didn't he trust that? "You *always* want something."

"This time I don't."

"Show me your hands."

He'd caught on to her finger-crossing trick, the one she used when she didn't want the lie to count.

Holding up both hands, she wiggled her fingers. "I'm not here because I want you to do something or buy something. I just came by to say hi."

"Huh."

She grinned. "Trust is an important part of our relationship. You really need to stop assuming the worst about me."

"It's only because I know you."

She laughed.

The sound washed over him, seeping inside and awakening things better left sleeping. When they were apart, he knew that being strong was best for both of them, but when they were together, sometimes he wanted more.

Buddy walked into the workshop and glanced around. Marissa went very still, waiting to see if the coyote would finally accept her. So far, he'd kept to himself, but this afternoon, he approached cautiously.

He paused about two feet away and sniffed.

"Hey, big guy," she said in a low voice. "You've lost the rest of your winter coat. You're gorgeous. Such a pretty face, too, although what with you being a guy, I should probably say you're handsome."

Buddy took another step toward her and pressed his nose close to her hand. Then he turned and bolted from the workshop.

Marissa laughed. "That was pretty cool. I think he's starting to accept me."

"He's cautious."

"As he should be. He's also amazing. I've always wanted a pet. Unfortunately my hours are crazy and it wouldn't be right to leave an animal alone for so long. Unless I got fish. But they're hard to cuddle."

He didn't want to think about that. "How's the auction going?"

"Good. We have less than a month to go. Donations are pouring in. People have heard about your bookcase and they're excited. We're going to start the bidding at four hundred dollars."

She sounded delighted. Aaron didn't burst her bubble by telling her that even a simple end table of his usually went for several thousand dollars. In an odd way, he liked the fact she had no idea how successful he was.

"Four hundred is great," he said.

"I think so. We get our books wholesale, so that's a lot of reading. Makes me happy." She pulled up a stool and plopped down. "How long have you been making furniture?"

"About five years."

"And why are you famous?" She winced. "I didn't mean that exactly how it came out. Your stuff is beautiful and all, but why are your pieces in magazines and not some other guy's?" She winced again. "I'm putting my foot in it here, but you know what I mean."

He chuckled. "Yeah, I know. Why did I get struck by lightning and not someone else?"

"Exactly."

He'd started making the furniture as a way to heal. Somehow working with wood seemed to ease the ache inside after losing his family.

"I was looking for a place to settle and this was as good as any," he said. "I started making tables and chairs. I'd always played around with this kind of thing, but I'd never done it seriously. One day I went to an auction to buy some old leather. I had this idea for a padded chair. There was a kid there, a photographer. We got to talking. It turned out he wanted to build a portfolio and I wanted some pictures taken of my work so I could start to sell it. We worked out a trade."

He settled on a stool. "In the process of showing

the pictures around New York, he gave them to a designer who was helping a friend dress a movie set. So they bought a couple of pieces, and when the stars were interviewed to publicize the movie, they used my furniture. A decorator for an upscale hotel chain saw the piece and called me, along with several of the cast members."

Her eyes widened. "Talk about a chain of events."

"You're right. In a year I went from barely paying the bills to having more work than I knew what to do with."

"It's amazing how a single event can make such a difference," she said, glancing at him from under her lashes.

He stared at her. "You're going somewhere with that."

"Not at all. I think it's great that your life was changed for the better. I had a similar thing happen. It didn't make me rich, but I'm successful." She leaned forward. "One moment, one person can make a difference."

He groaned. "You're killing me, you know that?"

"No, I'm not. I'm showing you the possibilities."

"Isn't teaching the woodworking class enough?"

"I don't know. That's for you to decide."

If only he could believe that. Marissa had a way of working her will on people that was nothing short of a gift. He just wasn't sure he wanted to be on the receiving end of her largess.

"Didn't you promise to leave me alone?" he asked.

"Not that I can recall. Besides, even though you'd rather eat glass than admit it, you like being part of the world. You're more comfortable on the fringes, but this is really okay with you."

He glared at her. "You don't know that."

"Am I wrong?"

Three simple words. An easy question. Aaron could answer it in his sleep. He preferred solitude and quiet and not being involved. He liked a day without surprises.

She watched him, her blue eyes bright with confidence and humor. He knew what she wanted him to say, what she *needed* to hear. It was as if her heart would wither and die without someone, somewhere, to save.

"Why are you doing this?" he asked. "Why aren't you married with a dozen kids to occupy your time?"

"I'm really busy. It's hard to establish a relationship because of that."

"Uh-huh. Now let's hear the real story."

She laughed. "You could at least pretend to believe me."

"I could, but I don't. Now talk."

She tucked her hair behind her ears. "I have horrible taste in men." She held up a hand to stop him from speaking. "I'm not kidding. I mean truly dreadful. I pick broken men and once they're mended, they dump me."

She sounded surprisingly cheerful, as if she accepted her destiny. At least this explained her attraction to him, though he wondered when she was going to figure out he couldn't be healed.

"Why?" he asked. "Why not regular guys who will make your life better?"

"I haven't a clue. Show me someone with a real job, a steady temperament and no serious baggage, and my heart barely beats. But put me in the path of someone in recovery, or a guy who's flirted with the law or is just an all-around loser, and I'm in heaven."

"Former bad girl seeks former bad guy?" he asked.

She frowned. "I hadn't thought of it that way. Maybe. I've done all the self-help books. I don't think it's a self-esteem issue, which still leaves an assortment of potential reasons. Growing up in foster care. Searching for a flawed partner so I can be the superior one. Or my personal favorite, which is my friend Ruby's theory."

"Which is?"

"I'm an idiot."

"I doubt that."

She was too smart. Which made him wonder why she'd avoided anyone who could make her happy.

"Just so we're clear," he said, "you know I'm past saving."

She smiled. "Gee, Aaron, is that an invitation?"

"Just the opposite."

"Your way of saying there's nothing between us?"

"There isn't."

But even as he spoke, he felt the attraction crackling in the air. It was like standing in an open area right before lightning struck. The air seemed charged; even the silence pulsed with anticipation.

"I mean it, Marissa. I'm not looking to get involved."

"Why?"

No way was he going there. "I have my reasons."

"I know. Deep, dark secrets and those wounded

eyes. Anyone else would run screaming in the opposite direction. A smart woman would."

"You're plenty smart."

"Not about men like you."

He felt buffeted by need. It came out of nowhere and consumed him. He couldn't think, couldn't speak, he could only want. She was so different from anyone he'd ever known. Fearless and vulnerable in equal measures. If he were any kind of gentleman, he would send her packing. But he'd always been something of a bastard.

Standing up, he moved toward her. He walked deliberately, giving her plenty of warning, plenty of time to bolt. Instead she swayed toward him in an erotic invitation he could no more deny than he could stop the tide.

He grabbed her shoulders and held her.

"This isn't a good idea," he growled.

"Tell me about it."

Then he kissed her.

CHAPTER
∽ SIX ∽

Marissa knew that kissing Aaron wasn't likely to appear as one of her ten most intelligent moves of the year, but she couldn't resist him. Not when he was so close to her and the heat of his body was searing her down to her bones.

She liked everything about him, especially the way he pulled her close and claimed her mouth. This wasn't like the last time. There was nothing delicate about his touch. He wasn't patient or seductive. Instead, he claimed her with an intensity that bordered on ravishment, and she found that suited her just fine.

His lips demanded even as he pressed his fingers into her back. She found herself grateful for the stool—it kept her from falling too hard and too fast, at least physically. She couldn't speak to the rest of her being.

He tilted his head and she did the same. When he nipped on her lower lip, her breath caught and her thighs began to tremble. When he swept his tongue across the place he'd nibbled, she parted her lips instantly.

He slipped inside with the practiced ease of a man intent on pleasing a woman. It was too much, she thought hazily; it would never be enough.

Wanting filled her. Wanting and need and desire and all those other delicious emotions she rarely allowed herself to feel. She wanted to beg him to take her right there on the workbench. She wanted to run out into the sunlight and pound her head against a tree until she forced some sense back into her brain. She wanted this moment to go on forever.

Instead she wrapped her arms around his waist and indulged herself by pressing her palms against his powerful muscles. She memorized the scent of his body and the way he tasted and how he moaned when she slid her own tongue into his mouth and stroked him.

Need grew, as did a sense of the inevitable. But just when she thought he would suggest taking things to the next level, he pulled back.

He rested his forehead against hers. At least he was breathing hard, she thought, pleased she wasn't the only one affected by what had just happened. When he cupped her cheek, she turned her head so she could kiss his palm. Finally he stepped back.

"This is crazy," he said.

"Probably."

He raised his eyebrows.

"Okay, definitely," she amended.

He turned to the window, then crossed to the open rear door and stared out at the forest.

"There are complications," he said. "Things you don't understand."

Her stomach took a quick and painful journey to her feet. "You're married."

He shook his head. "No. It's not like that."

"Then what's it like?"

He was silent for a long time. So long she began to think he wouldn't answer. Her mind raced with a thousand possibilities. He was sick. He was dying. He was gay.

"You're not gay, are you?"

That made him turn around and face her. He smiled slightly. "No. I'm not gay. But I can't do this."

"What?"

He motioned to her. "This."

Us. Them. A relationship. She wanted to ask why. She wanted to say that with chemistry like theirs, they were insane to ignore the possibilities. But for once, her nearly legendary courage failed her. She felt awkward and scared and more than a little off balance.

"Then what happens now?" she asked.

"I don't know."

"Want to come to my place for dinner one night this week?"

He stared at her. "Didn't I explain—"

"Actually, you didn't. You were very mysterious and woo-woo, but you didn't give me anything close to a reason."

He blinked. "Woo-woo?"

"You know what I mean."

"Not really."

"So?"

He drew in a deep breath. Her heart froze. She

desperately wanted him to agree, even knowing that if he did, she would be entering into dangerous territory. All that pain in his eyes might make him incredibly appealing to her, but it didn't make him a good candidate for a healthy relationship.

"What day is good for you?" he asked.

"Dinner, huh?" Ruby asked in a tone that said she thought the evening would be about a whole lot more.

"Yes. And just dinner. I want to take things slow with Aaron."

Her friend didn't look convinced. "You don't know fast from slow when it comes to men who are bad for you. So what's the guy's problem?"

Marissa looked up from the box of books she'd just opened—a donation from a former literacy student of hers. "Why does he have to have a problem?"

"Because you're interested in him," Ruby said wryly. "Come on. Spill. What is it? A prison record? Unpaid taxes? Six current wives?"

"It's not money and he says he's not married." Marissa stacked the books on the desk. "He's fine. Just a little reclusive."

"But?"

Marissa thought about bluffing her way through, but she'd never lied to Ruby and she was honestly confused.

"I don't know. I think he likes me." If his kisses were anything to go by, he liked her a lot. "He says he doesn't want a relationship, but then he accepted an invitation to dinner. He pulls back and moves forward in the same conversation."

"Commitment issues," Ruby said wearily. "The man's afraid love is a prison."

"I don't think so. There's something in his eyes. Something dark and sad. Like he's been seriously hurt."

Ruby set down a handful of picture books. "Girl, when are you going to get it? Pain in a man's eyes isn't a *good* thing. Run. Run now, while you still can. He's going to rip your heart out and chop it up into little pieces."

"No. I'm maintaining emotional distance. I'll be fine."

Her friend shook her head. "You call inviting him over to dinner, then mooning about him all week emotional distance?"

"I can still see him without having to worry about falling for him."

Ruby's brown eyes turned knowing. "Oh, it's like that, is it?"

Marissa frowned. "What do you mean?"

"It's too late. You're already crazy about this guy." She sighed. "You do like to lead with your heart."

"I don't..." Marissa was too surprised to do much more than stare. "I haven't fallen for him. I think he's nice and interesting and sexy, but that doesn't mean anything."

"Of course not."

"I'm serious."

"So am I. You're a goner." Ruby circled around the table in the library until she stood next to Marissa. "I hope he's all you want him to be," she said quietly. "I hope he makes you happy. But if he doesn't, you know I'll be here for you, right?"

Marissa was still too shocked to do much more than nod. No way had she fallen for Aaron. Not in such a short period of time. Of course she liked him. Who wouldn't? But serious feelings were something else. Besides, she'd promised herself she wouldn't make another bad choice. She was tired of giving and giving, only to end up alone.

But the white-hot burning in her heart warned her

that it might be too late to be making rational decisions where her feelings were concerned. Sometime, when she hadn't been paying attention, she'd started falling for a guy who went out of his way to tell her he wasn't interested.

"I wanted someone nice and normal," she said quietly.

Ruby shrugged. "Girl, you wouldn't know normal if it bit you on the butt. Look on the bright side. Maybe we're both wrong about Aaron. Maybe he's just a regular guy with a little history in his eyes. Maybe he's been dying to meet a woman just like you and settle down."

Marissa brightened. "You think?"

"It could happen."

Aaron arrived for his dinner with Marissa fifteen minutes late. He almost hadn't come. On the way over he'd nearly turned around twice, but in the end, he'd decided to keep the date, if only to tell her that he couldn't see her anymore.

She made him crazy, he thought as he pulled up to her small duplex and parked behind her battered import. She didn't have the good sense God gave a turnip, what with her running around and trying to rescue everyone. She wanted to make the world better and he wanted to be left alone. He was determined to make her understand things would never work out between them.

But first he wanted to see her. He wanted to breathe in the sweet scent of her body and listen to her laugh. He wanted to hear her explanation for a thousand different oddities of nature and whatever crazy plan she'd come up with for peace in the Middle East.

He wanted to touch her and taste her, which made him ache with guilt. Whenever those images filled his brain, he pushed them away. Liking was acceptable, but not wanting. Never that. He was only ever supposed to want Jilly.

Determined to get things cleared up once and for all, he slammed the truck's door closed and walked up the path. When he rang the bell, the sound seemed to echo.

A few seconds passed, then nearly a minute. He pushed the bell again. Nothing.

Aaron stepped back to make sure there were lights on in her side of the duplex. He knew he had the right house. Not only did he recognize the car, but there were crystals and sun catchers hanging from all the windows. Everything about the place screamed Marissa.

He knocked loudly and thought he heard a faint noise from within. Worry gripped him. When he tried the door, it was open, so he stepped inside and called out her name.

"In here," she said, her voice coming from the back of the house. "I'm sorry I'm not ready. I just need a little more time."

He followed the sound of her words through a cheerfully decorated living room into a bright kitchen. Children's artwork covered most of the walls. Something bubbled on the stove and delicious smells filled the room. But what most caught his attention was Marissa herself, sitting at a round table. Her skin was pale and damp, her eyes unfocused.

"What happened?" he asked as he crossed to her and touched her face. She was burning up with fever.

"I don't know. I started to feel a little tired earlier today and it's just been getting worse. Maybe I should have canceled. I'm kind of hot, but chilly, too, and I couldn't keep down lunch."

"The flu," he said as he walked to the stove and

turned off all the burners. "We need to get you into bed."

She blinked at him. "I think it would be better to take things more slowly than that, you know? Not that I don't think you're incredibly sexy and everything. But until I figure out why you have all that pain in your eyes, I have to be sensible."

When she finished talking, she put her head on the table. "I'm okay."

"I can see that."

He moved close and picked her up in his arms. She shrieked.

"What are you doing?"

"Making sure you don't pass out in the pasta." He started toward the stairs.

"But we're supposed to have dinner. I cooked."

"I'm sure it's delicious. I'll take a rain check."

She wrapped one arm around his neck and leaned her head against his shoulder. "What does that mean? Rain check. Why is there rain involved? Is it raining? I thought it was nice earlier. Did you think it was nice?"

There were two rooms at the top of the stairs. One seemed to be a home office and the other was a bedroom—pure girl. Pale colors, lots of flowers and frills and a four poster bed fit for a princess.

He set her on the edge of the mattress. "Where are your nightgowns?"

"Huh?" She blinked at him. "In the dresser." She pointed. "But I'm not really tired."

With that she collapsed back onto the mattress.

CHAPTER
～ SEVEN ～

"I'm saying that maybe I was wrong," Ruby said as she sat on the sofa beside Marissa.

Marissa half expected the roof to fall in. Not only was Ruby never one to admit that sort of thing, but what her friend was saying meant that Aaron wasn't like all the other men in her life. "The whole time?" she asked again.

"Every minute. You were out of it for nearly three days and the man never left your side. And let me tell you, you were doing some serious puking. It was gross."

Marissa didn't want to think about that. Her bout with the flu had laid her low for nearly ten days, but the first three had been the worst. She had few memories beyond feeling as if she'd already died and hearing Aaron's gentle voice promising her that things would get better.

"He ducked out twice a day to go check on that coyote of his and that was it," Ruby said. "He was worried, too."

"Wow." Despite still being a little weak and wobbly on her legs, Marissa couldn't help grinning. "So…"

Her friend smiled back. "He's got it bad. I can't believe after all this time, you finally picked someone right. He's smart and successful and easy on the eye. Plus, when the going gets rough, or in your case, when the going is some pretty nasty green stuff, he was right there. That's what I call a catch."

Marissa felt so happy, she wanted to float. "I should go see him. You know, to thank him."

"Uh-huh." Ruby looked amused. "I'm sure that's all you have on your mind. But a little advice. Wait until morning. For one thing, I don't want you driving at night just yet. You need to build your strength back up. For another, you're in some serious need of personal grooming."

Marissa fingered her lank hair. "You're right. I haven't had a shower in days. But I'll take care of all that in the morning, then go see him."

Her heart fluttered with excitement and the potential for finally finding her own happily ever after.

Aaron sat alone in the darkness, staring out the window. The promised storm had arrived and lightning cut through the inky blackness. He waited for the accompanying thunder, and when it came, he heard the angry judgment in the sound.

They were gone. The ghosts he'd come to count on as the last remaining tether to the life he'd once had faded. Two nights of drinking had done nothing to bring them back.

Pain cut through him. It was as if he'd lost Jilly and the baby all over again. They were gone, and he'd been the one to chase them away this time. They'd disappeared because of Marissa.

He closed his eyes and gave himself over to the recriminations. He should have left, he told himself for what must be the thousandth time. He should have called her friend and just walked away. But she'd been sick and he'd felt…worried.

No, he thought, opening his eyes and staring out into the storm. More than worried. He'd been frantic. When she'd passed out, he'd tasted terror. So he'd been right there with her for three days. He'd thought of nothing but getting her better. He'd forgotten, and that's what the ghosts couldn't forgive.

He turned his head, and when the next bolt of lightning illuminated the heavens, he saw the framed picture of his late wife. Jilly was laughing. She'd rarely been without a smile. He'd tried to comfort himself with that thought in the first year after her death. That she would have been smiling right up until the end. Singing to their baby and telling a story. She wouldn't have thought to imagine the worst. In her world, bad things never happened.

Bitter betrayal tightened around his chest like a tourniquet. He could barely breathe. He prayed for a stray bolt of lightning to crash through the roof of the house and strike him right then.

Bracing himself, he waited for the relief, but instead there was only the sound of the rain, then a cold dampness as Buddy sniffed his hand.

Aaron rubbed the coyote's ears. That's right, he told himself. He had Buddy to take care of. The animal would die without him, and he hadn't rescued him for that to happen. Reason returned, and with it, the list of his obligations. The woodworking class, the bookshelf he still had to finish.

He opened both hands. Buddy rested his head on one. Aaron closed the other in a fist.

Two worlds, he thought. What could have been and what was. The animal's fur was warm, and Aaron felt the steady beat of his blood pulsing through his body.

It was wrong to throw all this away because he'd lost his ghosts, he told himself. But he wanted to— he wanted to down to his soul.

Marissa washed her hair twice the next morning. She went through her wardrobe for the right outfit to wear to Aaron's. The man had spent three days with her while she looked like cat gack. She was determined to make a better impression when she showed up to thank him.

She still couldn't believe what had happened— that he'd stayed with her while she'd been so sick. Her heart told her that meant something important, something with the potential to change her life forever.

She couldn't seem to stop smiling as she walked into his shop later that morning. The open area looked much as she remembered—various pieces of furniture in different stages of assembly. The scent of spring and wood shavings filled the air. The heavy sliding doors at the back of the shop were open and she saw Buddy stretched out in a patch of sunshine.

Aaron stood by a bench. He wore safety goggles and was working some kind of sander. When he saw her, he flicked off the machine and pushed up his protective eyewear.

"Hi," she said, suddenly feeling shy and a little awkward.

"You're back on your feet," he said. "How do you feel?"

"About ninety percent. I still get a little tired by late afternoon, but otherwise I'm fine."

He nodded to the overstuffed chair in the corner. "Have a seat."

"Thanks."

Once she sat down, she let herself drink in his

appearance. Man, oh man, did he look good. Worn jeans that hugged narrow hips and long legs, a long-sleeved shirt rolled up to the elbow. He moved with that same easy grace that left her breathless.

"I wanted to thank you," she said, tucking her skirt around her knees. "For taking care of me. You didn't have to."

"You scared me," he admitted as he pulled up a stool across from her and sat. "You were pretty sick."

"It was going around the schools. I guess one of the parents in the reading program got it from her kids and gave it to me."

"Next time, look for a gift you can return."

She smiled. "Good point."

His dark gaze settled on her face and the contact was as potent as a touch. Her heartbeat increased, as did her breathing. Tension charged the air.

"Aaron," she began, but he cut her off with a shake of his head.

He stood and returned to the workbench, where he picked up a rag and began rubbing the legs of a half-built chair.

"Don't," he said, not looking at her anymore.

"Don't what?"

"Say whatever it is you're thinking."

"But I'm not…"

"Yes, you are." He kept his attention on his work. "I was married before. While I was in the service."

Marissa's breath caught as her muscles tensed. Married. She hadn't considered the possibility. She certainly didn't want to now, but if this was the reason for the shadows in his eyes, she had to know.

"What happened?" she asked. "Did you split up?"

He looked at her then, his expression both weary and heartsick. "No. I was away on deployment. She'd had our first child a couple of months before. Their car was hit by a drunk driver. The crash killed them both."

She didn't know what to think, what to say. What words could make any difference?

"I'm so sorry," she murmured at last. "You must have been devastated."

"More than that," he told her. "Destroyed. What I lost still haunts me. I never want to forget her…them." He swallowed. "I was overseas and I was supposed to go home the following week. I was getting out of the military, heading back to the States for good."

She ached for him and quickly rose. "Aaron."

He stepped back. "Don't. Don't touch me, don't try to fix this. You can't, and I don't want you to."

She nodded, even though she didn't understand. "How long?"

"Six years. But it could have been yesterday." He tossed the rag onto the bench. "I still love her. I'll always love her."

Marissa frowned. "Of course you will. What does that have to do with anything?"

"I don't want this," he said. "Not you or the kids or the town. I want to be left alone. I want you to go away and never come back."

His words hovered in the air like sawdust, then slowly filtered into her brain. At first the shock was so great that she didn't feel any pain.

"I don't understand," she whispered, even though she did.

"I won't betray what we had. I won't betray my family."

"By living? By caring about someone else?"

"You don't understand."

"Right. Because I've never lost anything and been left alone. We'll ignore the death of my parents when I was twelve. I'm sure my pain was wildly insignificant compared with yours," she said sarcastically. She didn't want to believe what he was saying, but he wasn't giving her a choice. She walked closer and put her hands on her hips.

"How dare you," she accused, feeling the anger fill her. Anger was safe, she thought. Anger would keep her breathing and moving and surviving. "How dare you retreat into your workshop and turn your back on the world. You have a responsibility."

He glared at her. "The hell I do."

"You're alive. That makes you a member of this society. Where do you get off retreating? Isn't it easy, just you and Buddy out here alone. Nothing to worry about except your next big fat check and getting the wood you need. All the time the rest of us are struggling to make a difference."

"Get out of here," he told her.

"I'm leaving. You bet. And if you really don't want to be a part of anything, I'll make sure it happens." She dropped her hands to her side. "I thought you were different. I thought you were one of the good guys. You claim to love your wife and child, but you certainly haven't honored them in their death. What does it say about your life with them that the only thing you want to do now they're gone is hide? Loving someone means opening your heart, and once you've done that, you can't ever close it again. Oh, sure, there's pain and a time of mourning, but eventually you're supposed to heal and move on."

She rubbed her hands along the chair leg. "It's perfect, Aaron. I'll give you that. But it's also cold and lifeless. Do you think your wife would be proud of you and what you've become? Do you think this is what she'd want as her legacy?"

He took a step toward her. "Don't you dare speak about my wife. You didn't know her."

"You're right. I didn't. But I imagine her to be beautiful and loving and someone I'd really like. That person would hate what you've become."

He leaned against the bench. "I told you not to try to save me. You should have listened."

"I'm listening now," she said. "I'm listening, and all I can say is that I feel sorry for you."

"Do you?" he asked, turning his attention back to her. "That's funny, because we're not all that different. I might hide in the dark, but you're also hiding. Only you do it in plain sight behind your projects and your loser guys."

She wanted to tell him he was wrong, that it wasn't like that. But when she opened her mouth, she found she couldn't speak. The pain she'd been avoiding crashed into her and nearly sent her to her knees. There was nothing to say, nothing to do but run.

CHAPTER
~EIGHT~

Marissa was as good as her word. The following week no one showed up for Aaron's woodworking class, and when he finished the bookcase for the auction, a man he'd never met came to pick it up.

No one visited him, no one called to ask him to speak anywhere or help with any cause. His life returned to the way it had been before—perfect solitude.

Even the ghosts came back. Nearly a week after Marissa had left, Aaron worked through the night, only to fall into an uneasy sleep just before dawn. He saw Jilly again. She was laughing. He heard the sound and it filled him with joy. He watched as she picked up their baby and danced with him across the small bedroom, but when he put out his hands to touch them both, they disappeared into the mist.

He awoke suddenly, his fingers grasping at air, and he knew then that the ghosts weren't real, and he was truly alone.

That night he drove to the library and stood outside Marissa's class. He heard her patient voice going over the night's lesson with her eager students. Adults read haltingly, stumbling over difficult words, but never giving up. She praised them and he heard the pride in their voices.

He returned to his large house on his isolated plot of land. Even Buddy had disappeared into the spring darkness.

Aaron walked from room to room, looking for something that wasn't there.

Around midnight, he heard a sound in the distance. The faraway wail of sirens made the hair on the back of his neck stand up. He walked to the big windows in his living room and stared toward the town. Flames licked up into the night.

Without thinking, he grabbed his truck keys and

hurried outside. Ten minutes later, he found himself parking at the edge of a massive fire.

Two apartment buildings seemed to be going up in flames. Firefighters swarmed around, dragging hoses and pulling people away from the danger. The smoke and heat were living creatures, sucking the oxygen from Aaron's lungs. People screamed, children cried. In the middle of the cacophony, he heard a young voice calling, "Mommy? Mommy, where are you?"

Turning, he saw a young boy dressed in pajamas. His hair stuck out in all directions, soot smudged one cheek, and he held a large picture book in his hand.

Recognition slammed into Aaron. "Christopher?" he asked, remembering the boy from the picnic.

At the sound of his name, the child looked up at him. "Who... Who are you?" he said with a sniff as he wiped the tears from his eyes.

"Aaron Cross. You read to me about a month ago. At the literacy picnic."

"My mommy hit her head. When she carried me out of the building. She fell down and didn't move and they took her away."

Aaron swore under his breath. How had the kid gotten separated from his mother?

"Do you have any brothers or sisters?" he asked. "Where's your dad?"

More tears spilled down the boy's cheeks. "I just have Mommy."

Without thinking, Aaron bent down and scooped the boy up in his arms. "Hey, it's going to be okay," he promised. "I'll help you find out what's going on."

He walked around the milling crowd looking for someone in authority. The firefighters were all too busy with battling the fire, and everyone from the apartment building seemed to be in a panic. Finally he located someone who would know exactly what to do.

Marissa stood at the edge of the disaster scene. She spoke into a cell phone while she gave directions to those around her.

"Maybe fifty families," she said into the phone. "The high school gym has the most space, plus there are showers and the home ec kitchens. Right. No. I've called them already. They're delivering cots and blankets. We'll have to get the word out for other supplies. I think most of these people have lost everything. Hold on."

She turned her attention to a couple of teens with clipboards.

"Start collecting names," she told the kids. "Find out who is missing and what family members need to be reunited. We'll have an information hotline up within the hour."

"You're kidding," the sleepy teenaged boy said. "How can you do that?"

She gave him a quick smile. "Practice. Now git."

The kids took off. Marissa completed her phone call, and as she hung up, he approached.

She looked tired, he thought. Dark circles shaded the area under her eyes and he had a feeling her weariness had nothing to do with the fire. He'd hurt her badly. First by making her think there was a possibility for the two of them to have a relationship, then by dismissing her in the cruelest way possible.

"What are you doing here?" she asked.

"I saw the fire." He paused. What *had* compelled him out into the night? "I wanted to help. Christopher here seems to have lost his mom." He briefly recounted the child's story.

Marissa shook her head. "At least there aren't that many hospitals to check. Can you take care of him until I can find out how she is?"

"Sure."

She looked more wary than pleased, which made sense. He thought of a thousand things he would like to say to her, but this wasn't the time. Instead he carried Christopher over to a relatively quiet grassy area by the parking lot and sat down.

The boy stared at him, and Aaron realized he didn't have a clue what to do.

"How you doing, sport?" he asked, feeling foolish even as he spoke the words.

The boy shrugged. Aaron struggled to think of something to say that wasn't frightening or stupid or a lie.

"I want my mom," Christopher said.

"I know you do, and I want to take you to her. But first my friend Marissa is going to find out where she is. Okay? That may take a little while. But I'm going to stay right here next to you. I'm going to keep you safe."

Big blue eyes stared at him. "Promise?"

Aaron made an X on his chest. "Cross my heart."

Christopher nodded, and at the same time he started to cry again. Not knowing what else to do, Aaron pulled him close and wrapped his arms around him.

"It's okay," he said, not sure if the words were true.

The tiny body shook. Aaron closed his eyes against the madness around them. For some reason, he thought of Jilly and their son and how he'd held the baby after he was born. Holding Christopher reminded him of all that he'd missed, but oddly enough, the pain wasn't as bad as he would have thought. Oh, sure, there was a sharpness to it, but he could survive.

He looked at the book the boy had dropped and reached for it.

"I remember this," he said. "It's all about cars. Boy, do I like cars. Always did." He opened the book and began to read.

Two hours later, the fire had been put out. About half the apartments had been destroyed and the rest were smoke and water damaged. Surprisingly, there had only been two injuries, and both had proved minor, which was why Marissa was looking for Aaron. She'd finally located Christopher's mother at a local hospital. The woman had a slight head injury and was expected to make a full recovery. The doctor wanted her to stay the night for observation, but he planned to release her in the morning.

Marissa had been relieved. Christopher would be happy and she could take him to the hospital on her way home. She would keep him overnight and then reunite him with his mother in the morning.

Everything had worked out better than she'd dared to hope. A fire in a crowded apartment building at night could have meant a devastating loss of life. Instead, everyone was going to be just fine.

Donations from the community had started to pour in and would continue. Once again, she'd made a difference and that felt really good.

Of course it wasn't enough to fill the gaping hole where her heart used to be, but she was getting used to that empty feeling in her chest. In time, she would stop loving Aaron and move on. Until then, she would put one foot in front of the other to carry on.

She rounded a corner and stumbled to a stop. Disbelief swept through her as she stared at the tall handsome man sitting on the damp grass, reading to several children by the emergency light from a nearby fire truck.

"You are the best baby kitten in the whole world," he read. "Your soft fur feels nice against my hand and your purr always makes me smile."

Christopher and a little girl were both snuggled up on Aaron's lap. Two slightly older kids leaned against him. Several teens were sitting around, holding younger children. And around them, dazed parents looked on with gratitude.

She must have made a sound because they all turned to look at her. She cleared her throat.

"The, uh, buses are here to take everyone to the shelter," she said. "If you have pets, animal control is offering foster care for as long as you need it."

The children scrambled up and headed toward their parents, except for Christopher, who clung to Aaron.

"I can take him," she said when the three of them were alone. She crouched down in front of the boy. "I talked to your mom. She's feeling just fine. I'm going to drive you to the hospital so you can see her, then we'll have a sleepover. In the morning, she'll come get you. How does that sound?"

"No!" Christopher buried his head in Aaron's shoulder. "Don't let her take me."

"I won't." Aaron hugged him close. "But I know you want to see your mom. What do you say the three of us go to the hospital together."

The boy sniffed. "Okay. Don't forget my book."

"I won't."

Aaron stood. "Does that work for you?"

She nodded as she rose. "Sure. But I don't understand. What are you doing here?"

"Helping."

"I got that. But why? I thought you wanted to be alone."

"I did." His beautiful dark eyes seemed to see into her soul. "I thought the ghosts were enough, but you were right. Jilly wouldn't be very proud of me right now."

Jilly. A beautiful name, she thought.

"I'm done hiding," he said. "I want to make a difference."

Good news, she told herself, refusing to hope. "That's great. There are a lot of local organizations looking for volunteers. I could hook you up with—"

He pressed his fingers over her lips. "I'll start up my woodworking class again and help out wherever you want, but that's not what I meant. I want to make a difference here. With you."

Marissa wanted to believe him, but she still hurt so much. "I guess we can talk about it later," she said.

* * *

The morning of the auction dawned perfectly clear. Marissa knew, because she'd been awake to see it. Nerves had kept her from sleeping. Nerves and anticipation.

This was the biggest event she'd ever planned. So much was riding on the success of the day. She was supposed to give a big speech right before they auctioned off Aaron's bookcase and she'd rewritten her text about four million times. As of ten minutes ago, she still didn't have it right.

"I need to concentrate," she told herself as she waited for the second pot of coffee to brew. How could she? Between all the last-minute details occupying her mind and the way Aaron kept popping up in her brain, she felt as scattered as a balloon in a twister.

Aaron. He'd been as good as his word. Two weeks ago he'd started up his classes once again, had shown up for literacy training and invited her out to dinner three times. The impending auction meant she hadn't been able to accept, but she'd been tempted.

Even knowing how he'd hurt her, she'd wanted to see him again, be alone with him. She'd longed to hear him say she mattered, that they belonged together. But would he? Was his transformation about his need to heal the world, or was it about them?

She was willing to admit to more than a little fear on that front. On her good days, she told herself it was important to know where they stood. On her bad days, she wanted to run away and hide.

Promptly at seven-fifteen the phone began to ring as people called with questions about setup and deliveries. She got out of the house at nine and by noon was fighting panic and a headache.

By two, the high school auditorium was standing room only. By four, they'd sold everything but Aaron's bookcase. Marissa checked her makeup in the tiny cracked mirror backstage as she prepared to head out to deliver her speech on the Motheread/Fatheread® program.

"It's not here." Ruby ran up to Marissa and grabbed her arm. "Aaron's bookcase. It's not here."

"What? I saw it this morning."

"Maybe, but it's gone now."

Marissa stared at her friend. "Stolen? But who would do that? I don't…"

The auctioneer began his introduction.

"You're on," Ruby said, pushing her toward the front of the stage. "You're going to have to stall them while we figure out what we're going to do."

"Don't stall anything," Aaron said as he approached.

Marissa turned and stared at him. "Did you hear? Your bookcase is missing."

He smiled a warm, sexy smile that made her heart flutter and her mouth go dry. "I took it home. It wasn't right."

"I don't understand."

"This program is worth a whole lot more than just a bookcase."

He jerked his head over his shoulder. Behind him, men were carrying in chairs, tables and sofas. She couldn't believe it.

"Aaron, I appreciate the gesture, but we can't possibly sell all that. The people around here don't have enough money."

"I know. I'm holding back a couple of chairs for local bidders only, but the rest of it will go onto the Internet auction."

She blinked. "The what?"

"I've been setting it up all week. I sent a mailing

to my clients, informing them of the auction. Most of them are sitting in front of their computers, ready to start buying. I'm figuring we'll get close to five hundred thousand for the lot."

Ruby gasped. "That's going to buy a lot of books."

"My thoughts exactly," he said.

Marissa didn't know what to think. "Why are you doing this?"

"Because someone I care about very much once told me that even a single individual can make a difference. I finally figured out she's right." He touched her cheek. "That's your cue."

"What? Oh." Marissa smoothed the front of her dress and stepped onto the stage. Everyone in the auditorium applauded her entrance.

"Without this little lady here, we wouldn't have much of a program at all," the auctioneer said.

Marissa walked to the microphone and smiled. "Thank you all so much. I've just found out there's going to be a change in the program. There's no Aaron Cross bookcase to bid on."

Several people groaned.

"Instead we're going to auction off an entire collection."

As the furniture was carried on stage, she explained about the online bidding.

"This all goes for a good cause," she said. "Most of you know how the Motheread/Fatheread® program has changed so many lives in our community. What you may not know is that we're reaching beyond our community to men and women in desperate need of a second chance. Volunteers are working with parents in prison. Most of those incarcerated can't read very well, if at all. They're away from their children and they don't know how to be good parents. Our program gives them the opportunity to learn a valuable skill— reading—and to use that skill to become better mothers and fathers. We're teaching them to communicate, to understand what their children need from them. For many, the love of a child is incentive enough to find a new and better life after being released."

She looked around at the familiar faces in front of her. "I didn't grow up in a big family. I was raised in foster care, where no one had the time to read me a story. So I know what it's like to wish for that connection. For all of you who are willing to give just a little so others can know the pleasure and wonder of reading to their children, I thank you."

Applause filled the auditorium. One by one, the people rose until they were all standing. Suddenly the stage filled as the volunteers joined her, clapping and cheering.

Marissa didn't know what to say, where to go. Gratitude filled her. She glanced around and saw Aaron joining in the applause.

As she looked at him, she saw that the pain was gone from his eyes. She'd spent the last two weeks pushing him away and he'd continued to show up. That had to mean something.

Without thinking about the thousand or so people watching, she walked over to him.

"Why are you still here?" she asked.

"Because there's nowhere else I'd rather be."

"Than at the auction?"

He smiled. "Than with you. I meant what I said, Marissa. You got it exactly right. I've been living my life the easy way. Staying alone, mourning. What kind of a legacy is that? I'll always love Jilly and my son, but that doesn't mean my heart is closed. There's plenty more love in there for a wonderful woman who constantly pushes me to be my best. I want to be there for you. I want to be the one person you're willing to lean on. I want to love you and look after you—if you'll have me."

He moved closer. "You're so busy taking care of others, you don't bother taking care of yourself. The way I see it, you're in need of a good rescuing, and I'm just the man to do it."

She was too stunned to speak. This was everything she'd ever dreamed of Aaron saying to her, and yet she couldn't seem to form any words for a response.

"Kiss him!" somebody yelled.

"What?"

She turned and saw they were the center of attention. Even the auctioneer watched eagerly.

"You heard the nice man," Aaron said with a grin. "Kiss me."

"Why should I?"

"Because you love me nearly as much as I love you. Because you've spent your whole life falling for the wrong guy, and this time you've got it right. And because you want to."

She started to laugh. "When did you get so smart?"

He picked her up and swung her around. "The day you walked into my shop and started taking over my life."

She sighed as he set her back on the ground. "That was a good day," she said, wrapping her arms around him.

"This one's better."

He dropped his head and kissed her. Marissa heard cheering in the background, but she couldn't be bothered to see who it was. Not when Aaron was there, holding her, wanting her. Loving her.

She drew back. "Did I tell you I love you?"

He cupped her cheek. "With everything you do."

"All right, you two," Ruby ordered. "Let's get off this stage so they can finish up the auction."

Once they were backstage, Aaron pulled Marissa into a corner. "I want to marry you," he said. "Let me take care of you, love you. For always."

She nodded, her throat too tight to speak. He wasn't just offering her his heart—he was offering the one thing she'd been looking for all her life.

Home.

Dear Reader,

For so many of us, books are magic. They are an escape, a way to learn, to experience a place, a time, or even a galaxy far, far away. Reading is something we look forward to on a long plane ride, on vacation or at the end of a stressful day. But for those who can't read, life is difficult. And for those who must admit to their children they don't know how to read, life is filled with shame.

The Motheread/Fatheread® program helps parents with literacy and Dena Wortzel has spearheaded this program in Wisconsin.

Dena is a great advocate of reading. Like many of us, she read constantly as a child. Books were like good friends, only they didn't have to be in by dark. Dana believes the act of reading is part of being a family. That parents reading to children is vital for the intellectual and emotional growth of the child. The child reading with the parent offers a wonderful connection that bonds the family together.

But Dena does more than talk about the importance of reading. She gets involved. She teaches the principals of Motheread/Fatheread® to inmates in the Wisconsin correctional system.

I loved talking to Dena and using her life as an inspiration for this story. We share a love of words and reading. Dena is amazing—a true example for us all. Writing for this project was an honor and a privilege.

Happy Reading

Susan Mallery

GLORIA GILBERT STOGA
∽—PUPPIES BEHIND BARS—∽

W hat can be said about Gloria Gilbert Stoga, who routinely sells hardened convicts on raising puppies in their prison cells? Not only that, the tiny 110-pound marathon runner has the inmates rolling on the ground, crowing like a rooster and dancing—all to train the pups.

Gloria is president and founder of Puppies Behind Bars, a nonprofit organization that uses prison inmates to train puppies to become service dogs for the physically disabled or explosive-detection dogs for law enforcement. Through her dreams and efforts, Gloria has been able to provide a new "leash" on life for both the inmates participating in the program and the eventual recipients of the working dogs.

For the disabled who receive the specially trained

dogs, Puppies Behind Bars gives them confidence and freedom to travel independently with safety and dignity. For the law enforcement officer who receives a trained explosive-detection canine, it provides a partner that helps keep society safe. For the inmates who nurture and train these special animals, Gloria's program provides a sense of purpose, accomplishment and responsibility by allowing them to care for a small, dependent—not to mention wriggly—life. Prison inmates contribute to society rather than take from it.

"The knowledge that we're doing something to help is a sense of great pride," says Gloria.

The story begins back in 1990 when Gloria and her husband adopted a Labrador retriever from one of North America's most prestigious guide-dog schools, Guiding Eyes for the Blind. Arrow had been on his way to becoming a guide dog, but was released from the program for medical reasons. Gloria started reading about Arrow's training and was amazed to discover how much time, effort, love and money— $25,000—goes into each guide dog. She also learned there was a shortage of guide dogs in the United States.

Gloria wanted to find some way to help the cause. But how?

An idea turns real

It wasn't until Gloria's sister cut an article out of a magazine telling the story of Dr. Thomas Lane, a vet in Florida who started the first guide-dog prison program, that Gloria found her answer. But starting a similar program in New York, New Jersey and Connecticut meant leaving her job on New York mayor Giuliani's Youth Empowerment Services Commission and heading out into a great unknown. Would anyone give her the dogs to train? Could inmates really be responsible enough to work with these dogs full-time? How would the puppies learn to be guide dogs if they were never exposed to a normal, non-prison environment? Was Gloria crazy to even launch the project?

It was finally Gloria's husband who gave her a not-so-gentle nudge.

"I talked about it for two years, and after two years my husband finally said, 'Gloria, you either have to shut up or do something about it,'" she says with a laugh.

She quit her job and got down to work.

Today sixty-two women and eighty-one men in seven different prisons in three different states are currently raising ninety dogs to be either potential service dogs or explosive-detection dogs. Close to 85 percent of these pups pass their tests to go on to get further training.

The program works. Puppies Behind Bars now has 303 working dogs helping people every day. Eighty-three are guide dogs throughout the United States, and 188 are explosive-detection canines in the U.S. and abroad. Eighteen are service dogs, including nine who have gone to soldiers who have come home wounded from Iraq or Afghanistan (under a new initiative Puppies Behind Bars calls Dog Tags: Service Dogs for Those Who've Served Us). Fourteen others function as companion and therapy dogs for blind children. They're a well-traveled bunch. One former prison puppy now works to keep the president of Egypt safe. Another was at Pope John Paul's funeral. Other dogs are used at Kennedy and LaGuardia airports. There are also Puppies Behind Bars dogs at the United Nations.

Lucie, one of the first guide dogs to come out of the program, gave a retired registered nurse, who was imprisoned in her home after losing her vision following a stroke, the gift of independence and mobility.

No wonder one of the inmate dog trainers currently in the program calls Gloria "an unsung national treasure, the poet laureate of puppies."

A dog's life

Certainly inmates at the maximum security prisons who take part in the Puppies Behind Bars programs must be screened carefully. The inmate has to have a clean prison disciplinary record for at least a year, must participate in facility programs and be considered reliable by prison officials. He or she must also have at least two years left to serve before potential parole, since dogs are with the inmates for a year and a half.

Once chosen for the program, puppies live in their cell and the trainers attend weekly puppy classes, and complete homework and exams. The trainers also swap the puppies so the dogs will be accustomed to different people and environments.

But dogs in training need to get out of the prison system, too. A weekend puppy-sitting program means the puppies stay with volunteer host families in the suburbs surrounding the prisons and in New York City at least six times a month. Some of these visits are for several hours, while others are overnight "furloughs."

While the dog's recipients and inmates obviously benefit from the program, inmates' families also gain plenty, says Gloria. After the puppies find their way into their lives, inmates finally have something positive to talk about. They share their puppy's reaction to the first snowfall or how cute they are when they dream. Family and friends see that the person behind bars is giving back to the community.

"It strengthens family bonds, because there is a common positive thing to talk about. Families can feel proud of their incarcerated loved ones instead of just feeling embarrassed," she says.

Even dogs that do not make it all the way through the training program after they are released from the inmates' care go on to help people. These dogs are given to families with blind children. One boy, a quadriplegic blind child who received "Jack" as a pet, is now able to move his arms to pet him.

"We do effect change. I don't mean to say that lightly or with arrogance, but we really do affect a lot of people's lives," Gloria says.

PUPPIES BEHIND BARS

For more information visit www.puppiesbehind-bars.com or write to Puppies Behind Bars, 10 East 40th Street, 19th Floor, New York, NY 10016.

KAREN HARPER
∽ Find the Way ∽

❧—KAREN HARPER—❧

New York Times bestselling author Karen Harper is a former high school and college English teacher. Winner of the 2005 Mary Higgins Clark Award for her outstanding novel *Dark Angel*, Karen is the author of fourteen romantic-suspense novels and three historical novels, as well as a series of historical mysteries. Karen and her husband, who divide their time between Columbus, Ohio, and Naples, Florida, love to travel both in the U.S. and abroad. For additional information about Karen and her novels, please visit www.karenharperauthor.com.

CHAPTER
∼ONE∼

"**Y**ou mean you're going to get a Seeing Eye dog?" her mother demanded, her voice rising. "But you don't even like dogs, Alexis. You've always been a cat person!"

"I'm not looking for another pet. It isn't like that at all. And they're called guide dogs, not Seeing Eye dogs."

Alexis heard her mother flop into the beanbag chair. She had been expecting surprise at best, scolding at worst when she'd made her announcement. She knew her mother wasn't going to accept this bolt from the blue so easily. No, that would not be like Jillian Michaels at all, so there was surely more protest coming.

Her mother had been visiting for two days, and it had taken Alexis this long to mention her big decision. Before she was permanently blinded by a head injury when she fell down a flight of stairs while fleeing a stalker, Alexis Anne Michaels had been an independent twenty-six-year-old on her own in the big city of Elizabeth, New Jersey, just a short hop to both Newark and Manhattan. But these last two years, everything had been sadly different.

She fought to keep calm, to explain things well. "Guide dogs are raised and trained to be gentle and would never jump up on anyone or hurt them. It's like a partnership." She stared at the spot where she judged her mother's eyes to be. The memory of that pert, pretty face suddenly illumined the darkness like a TV being turned on.

Before her mother could say more, Alexis plunged on. "These dogs are only part-time pets because they're working dogs when in harness. They're intelligent and well behaved, so much so, I hear, that I can keep Chaucer, too." She bent over to pet the gray-and-white longhair Persian rubbing against her ankles.

It had taken the poor cat only one day to learn she could no longer put herself in her mistress's path without getting kicked or causing a tumble. Only when Alexis was sitting, standing or lying down did Chaucer approach her now.

"I know you haven't liked using your white cane," Jillian said, "but I thought you were considering my suggestion that you move back home with me for good. I can see why you can't cope with a busy, crowded neighborhood in a huge city. You need to be home with me where it's much more quiet—and safe. Since your father's no longer with us, I can devote myself to taking care of you, to getting you here and there, just like old times before you could drive. You know, my old soccer-mom days."

"We have to accept that my blindness means there are no more old times, only new ones," Alexis reminded her mother. "You have your friends at home, your bridge and reading clubs. Now that Daddy's gone, you're still finding your way into a new life, too."

Alexis opened the crystal of her braille watch and felt the hands and numbers. Nearly five o'clock; she wanted to fix soup and a sandwich before her mother set out on her two-hour train ride home. Besides, if Alexis had something to do with her hands, she wouldn't wring them. Her mother didn't want to admit that anything in their lives had changed. Not that her husband had dropped dead from a heart attack two years ago at the age of sixty-two, or that four months later, a sick stalker's obsession had resulted in an accident that had ruined her daughter's sight.

At first, after two tragedies so close together, Alexis had been very willing to let her mother take care of her in her small New Jersey hometown. But she'd felt like a child, and despite fears that her stalker might turn up again, she had returned to E-town, as the locals called it. After all, Blair Ryan, the detective investigating her case, had eventually concluded that "the perp" had fled the area.

Still, Alexis had changed apartments—with the help Detective Ryan and another officer had insisted on giving her. She knew they were still trying to trace Len Dortman, the man who had stalked and assaulted her. Dortman wouldn't find her at the high school where she'd taught either, because she'd had to take a leave of absence, which she was afraid would be permanent unless a guide dog could work miracles.

Previously Alexis had shared a renovated town house with a friend, another high-school teacher, who'd been married last summer. The place was too expensive for Alexis to afford on her own, had a loft, a basement and a curving staircase. Her new apartment was smaller and cheaper and all on one floor, though she'd had to learn its layout since she'd never seen it.

She'd been here over a year now, and the fact that nothing had happened surely meant that Len Dortman had fled with no clue where she was. Otherwise, his disturbing phone calls, the bizarre letters and the all-night vigils he'd made outside her old place would have started up again by now. Alexis had had a lot of time to memorize her new place. She supported herself with disability checks and income from tutoring students in her apartment. Despite her visual impairment, she helped them with reading comprehension and composition skills to prepare for college entrance exams. She also graded essays for two other teachers by having her talking scanner read the works aloud, then she dictated her corrections and suggestions.

During her days of deepest depression, it had boosted her spirits that her former students had taken up a collection and bought her software that read e-mail to her. Alexis was getting more proficient with braille, but only as an aid, so she relied on talking books a lot. For ten weeks, a special bus had picked her up and taken her to a center for courses that taught her to trust her senses of touch, smell and hearing. But, even with all that and her white cane, her sense of independence eluded her. After barely escaping being hit by a truck that cut a corner too close, Alexis feared going out on her own.

"Come on into the kitchen while I fix us a light early supper," she said, gently moving Chaucer aside with one leg.

"Here, let me take care of that," Jillian said, popping up so quickly she created a draft.

"Mother, what have you been buying me all these fancy talking devices for if you don't let me open my own cans?" Alexis felt along the familiar cupboard shelf for the can she wanted. She'd had them placed in a specific order, but her mother must have scrambled them.

"Well, it's one thing to tell a tuna can from a soup can," Jillian said, following Alexis to the door of the narrow galley kitchen. "But those little things I bought online will tell you exactly what kind of soup and play a helpful little message, too. How did you ever do it on your own, or do you just eat potluck?"

"Didn't you see these braille markers I attach to the tops with rubber bands? I can label them that way, just as I do my clothes, to know what's what. I just remember which marking is which," she explained, then realized her mother must have removed her braille markers from the cans and replaced them with these new doodads. Alexis jumped when she touched the tiny button on the magnetic cap and it spoke.

"Hi, darling, your mother here," the recorded message said. "This is a can of cream of mushroom soup, which goes well with almost any sandwich. You can pick out veggies by touch to make a salad, but be careful cutting things up. You might want to doctor this soup up a bit by add——"

Though Jillian had spoken quickly, the message ended in midword. *You might want to doctor this up* . . . echoed in Alexis's mind as her mother came over and reached past her to play the messages on the other cans, joking lamely that living at home with a *doggedly* helpful mother would be better than getting a dog. But Alexis was hardly listening.

Doctored up, she thought. The best ophthalmology specialists and surgeons had not been able to doctor her up to restore her sight. Her fall had caused a stroke, which had affected her optic nerve but nothing else.

Her relationship with her stalker had started normally enough. Len Dortman was the assistant custodian at the school where Alexis taught. He hung around a bit too much, always trying to help her, but that was all. At first she'd tried to be nice, then to put him off, then to avoid him. When she'd told him to leave her alone, Dortman had stalked her for weeks, though she hadn't realized it at first. Eventually Alexis had phoned the police; an officer ordered Dortman to completely avoid her. When he didn't, she'd obtained a restraining order. The fallout from that got him fired; evidently he'd tried to assault her as she jogged. She still had memory loss from the day of the attack, but she must have fought him off and run. Either he'd pushed her or she'd fallen down a flight of steps at the old amphitheater in the park. Two teenagers looking for some privacy had found her and called 911. But the police had not located Dortman, who had left his apartment and not returned. Alexis prayed he never would.

Though she dreaded recalling that final confronta-
tion with Dortman, Alexis had tried to get the memory
back. Detective Ryan surmised what happened when
a witness later came forward to say he'd seen both the
victim and her stalker running but thought they were
having some sort of race. The last thing Alexis could
recall of that dreadful day was opening her mail at
home after school and finding the videotape she'd
ordered of Kenneth Branagh's *Hamlet* to use in class.
Branagh was in a photo on the front, all in black,
holding poor Yorick's skull. Two days later, she'd
wakened in the hospital to voices and sounds, because
her eyes were bandaged. The first voice she'd heard
was her mother's, followed by the deep, sure tones of
Detective Ryan. Alexis realized her world had gone
dark, and ever since, she'd seen only sliding, shifting
black-gray shapes.

How she longed to stride outside these narrow
walls with confidence. To be her graceful, athletic self
again, not to walk fearfully and bump into things and
look like a drunk or a klutz. To get back some semblance of her once-independent life, and that included
figuring out if the attention Blair Ryan still paid her
was professional or personal. The nightmare of the

stalker had damaged more than her vision; she had terrible issues with trusting men now.

Yet just thinking about Blair made her stomach cartwheel. Kenneth Branagh and even Sean Connery couldn't compete with Blair's rich, resonant voice. Alexis had never seen his face and had no intention of asking him if she could touch it, so she always pictured him as Kenneth Branagh, all in black. She did know that Blair was about six inches taller than her five foot six, with a compact, strong build. She'd leaned on his arm more than once, and he'd hugged her the day she'd been released from the hospital. Her heart pounding, she'd hugged him in return, but she had to wonder now, why did he keep coming back?

She figured that if it wasn't pity, it must be guilt that he hadn't found Dortman, that the case wasn't closed. And that's why she'd turned down Blair's invitation for dinner and dancing—dancing, no less!

"How much does a guide dog cost anyway?" her mother asked, startling Alexis from her thoughts.

"Twenty-five thousand dollars to raise and train, but," she added hastily when she heard her mother gasp, "absolutely free to those who qualify and need them. I need one, Mother. I really do. And I've agreed to accept one raised in a prison, Eastern Correctional Facility. It's not far from here."

"What? That's a maximum-security prison!" Jillian stepped forward to grasp her by both arms. "You won't know who's handled that dog, or what's happened to it that might make it—well, snap."

"I've been told these dogs are beautifully trained and gentle." With the hand not holding the soup can, Alexis grasped her mother's wrist. She hoped she was looking her straight in the eye. "The dogs are raised under a strictly supervised program called Puppies Behind Bars. The whole thing was the inspiration of a woman who's had great success with it since she founded it in 1997."

"But a murderer could have raised that dog," her mother whispered, as if that very felon might be eavesdropping.

"The program's founder used to think we should just lock inmates up and throw away the key. But she's proved that having them raise these puppies and give them basic obedience training before they go on to guide dog school has helped the inmates too. The program is not only assisting the blind, but showing that inmates are people who can make a contribution and change their ways."

"Alexis Anne Michaels, don't you realize that the person who raised your dog could be just like that horrible man who did *this* to you?"

"This particular prison has only women, and this is not up for a vote. I've applied and had a phone interview already, so that's that. I hope you'll support me in this and——"

Her mother's grip on her upper arms loosened. But to Alexis's relief, she didn't back away or protest further. Instead, Jillian hugged her hard, and Alexis clasped her mother in return. They stood, holding tight, one in relief—the other, probably, with regret. But they both laughed when the talking can of soup Alexis still held was jostled and sang out, *"Hi, darling, your mother here..."*

Tina Clawson, inmate #81A1268 at the Eastern Correctional Facility for Women, aged thirty-two, was serving a ten-year sentence for cocaine possession with intent to distribute. She knelt on the hard concrete, cuddled her ten-month-old black Labrador retriever and cooed, "Puppy, puppy, puppy. I love my good girl Corky!"

Tina picked up Corky's sopping-wet duck squeaky toy and heaved it again. The retriever's paws skidded on the concrete before she got enough traction to scamper after it, yipping in delight.

"Get it, Corky!" Tina shouted over the encouraging cries of the other puppy raisers to their dogs. "Get that big bad toy and bring it back to Mama!"

She did think of herself as Corky's mom, and cherished every minute with her just as she had with her first dog, Sterling, a chocolate Labrador retriever. That was the only downer with this Puppies Behind Bars program. After bonding with the puppies, loving and training them for sixteen months, the inmates gave them up so they could attend guide dog school or get training to become Explosive Detection Canines, called EDCs. The few dogs that didn't fit either program became release dogs given to families with kids who were blind.

The first dog Tina had raised went to a person who was blind, but this time the prison had puppies that would become bomb sniffers. After the 9/11 tragedy, a lot more canines were needed for domestic- and even foreign-security assignments.

Five other female inmates exercised their dogs in

the puppy rec area they visited three times a day. *Jollying*, the program's founder had called this playtime when she'd gotten Puppies Behind Bars under way here. Now the once-a-week training classes—training for raisers and dogs—was taught by someone else. Still, the founder herself had interviewed the inmates and made certain they understood and accepted their responsibilities before they'd signed a contract with PBB.

Corky scampered back again, proudly dropping her toy at Tina's feet. She looked up for approval, then lowered her head and continued to stare at the stuffed cloth duck as if she had just brought in a real bird for a hunter. That desire to please a handler as well as the search-and-retrieve instincts would help to make Corky a successful EDC.

Overwhelmed with love for the little mite, Tina gently wrestled with the bundle of energy. They even butted heads, Tina's spiky blond hair against Corky's silky, ebony coat.

"Corky, sit," Tina said.

The dog obeyed. Corky understood all the basic commands like *sit, stay* and *heel,* Tina thought proudly. Tina had felt like a failure herself, but through her puppies, she was gaining confidence that at last she was doing something right.

"Only ten more minutes, ladies and canine companions," Ellen, the officer with them, announced with a grin. Ellen liked watching the cavorting puppies as much as anyone else, but puppy rec was the only time Tina had ever seen her laugh.

How Tina wished her two kids could have a puppy, but her widowed mama was barely making ends meet keeping them in food and clothes. Tina's husband had died when he'd OD'd on crack, so when Tina got sent here, their grandma was the only person that little Larry, age eight, and Sandy, seven, had in this world. Tina had a sister, Vanessa, who could have taken the kids, but she'd argued with their mama years ago and moved who knew where.

And though Tina was totally off drugs and would never use again, it would be nearly four more years till she got out of here. *Four more years...four more years,* a chanting voice repeated in her head. She was so scared something would happen to her kids while she was stuck in here.

The puppy raisers had been told that very first day, "Never set up a dog for failure, because we build on success." Tina had tried, God knows she'd tried, but when you were just a big bundle of failures and regrets yourself, it sure was a tough thing to learn confidence and then teach it to a dog. Being told about "Sterling's sterling success" in guide dog school had helped bolster her fragile confidence.

"Tina!" Ellen called to her when she'd put Corky back on her leash and was ready to head to the prison laundry room to work. Corky loved to watch the clothes and water in the big, front-loading washers swish around. "Warden Campbell wants a word with you."

Now, *that,* Tina thought, was never good news. "Corky, come," she commanded.

As Tina preceded Ellen down the long corridor toward the warden's office, other officers and inmates said hello to her and Corky. Though Tina didn't break stride, several stooped to give the puppy a quick pat. Having these animals around made everyone happier and calmer, but not Tina right now. She felt so uptight she could throw up.

Tina had heard that Warden Marian Campbell had been against the PBB program at first, but she was gung ho for it now, especially since it made the prison atmosphere better. Sometimes the warden even let the dogs visit women who were ready to walk into their parole hearings because it calmed them down. Sterling had visited the domestic-violence training classes more than once, since having a dog there seemed to help the women open up and share their feelings. One of those inmates had told her that Sterling, who was usually calm, used to get a little upset if the women became distraught. It was like the dog could feel someone's pain, Tina thought.

Right now, her own feelings were on hold—iced up, just the way she used to feel all the time before she became a puppy raiser. To help herself face the warden as she entered the office, she scooped Corky up in her arms and held her tight.

"Have a seat, Tina," Warden Campbell said. Tina obeyed, scooting back into the hard, wooden chair, with Corky on the floor at her side. The warden came around her big, cluttered desk and perched on the edge of it, looming over Tina. The woman had striking, high cheekbones and smooth skin the color of milk choco- late. Though she could be really stern, the puppies had always made the warden smile. But not now.

The warden frowned. "I'm afraid I have some sad news, Tina."

"Not one of my kids?" Tina cried. She knew she shouldn't interrupt, but she couldn't help it. "They're hurt? Worse?"

"You're an honor inmate making great strides here, Tina, so I've decided to tell you this myself. I'm sorry, but your mother had a massive heart attack last night and did not survive. Your children——" she glanced down at a folder open on her desk behind her "——a girl and a boy, both minors, were taken in by the neighbors for the night. But because there is no known next of kin, they have been remanded into the custody of children's services, which will try to place them in foster homes. There is no other next of kin, is there?"

"My sister Vanessa, but she's——moved somewhere 'fore I got in here. She'd take them though. She loves kids, loved my kids…" Her voice choked on a sob.

It seemed to Tina as if another woman had said that to the warden. She should have been there with Mama and the kids. *She should be there now!* Fury poured through her. Anger and hatred at herself, at the world. Mama had been so good to take the kids when their parents had let them down. It had been a real burden at her age. A heart attack——it was Tina's fault, and now the kids would be with someone who was not kin.

"Tina, I'm so sorry for your loss," the warden said, and leaned forward to squeeze her shaking shoulder before briefly touching Corky's head. "I've arranged for someone else to take your place in the laundry room today if you need time alone."

Alone. When would she ever see Larry and Sandy again? They'd forget about her by the time she got out. The prison wasn't that far from her mama's home, but children's services or new foster parents wouldn't bring Larry and Sandy here for a visit like Mama had. And was there money to bury Mama proper, and was there money for stuff the kids needed?

Tina had never felt more of a failure—again. *Don't set the puppies up for failure but for success...* She sat in the chair in the warden's office, silently sobbing, while the puppy licked her hand.

CHAPTER
❧ TWO ❧

It was a great spring day, so Detective Blair Ryan sat at a sidewalk table and ate his tortilla. The taverna made it just the way he liked it, with Spanish onions, red peppers, guacamole and lots of meat. He swiped some salsa off his chin, then took a swig of his soft drink.

He kept his back against the wall—instinct from officers' training and also his year in Afghanistan. This wasn't Kabul, though these could be mean streets, too. With the large influx of Latinos, the area was making a transition from traditional blue-collar to ethnic-hip. It was also popular because of affordable rents, despite its proximity to Manhattan.

A hometown boy from nearby Newark, Blair liked E-town and chose to live here. This neighborhood especially was a great mix of Latino, Polish and Indian cultures.

Blair tossed the last of his crust to a watchful seagull, one of many that flew in from Newark Bay, where container ships were being loaded and unloaded. It seemed like just yesterday that his mom had brought him and his sister, Kate, down here on Saturdays when their dad was working—almost all the Ryan men had been cops—to eat in a restaurant overlooking the loading docks and harbor. But cancer had claimed Kate when she was only nine, and he'd never gone near that restaurant again.

He tossed his trash in a KEEP OUR CITY CLEAN can and strolled down the street toward the renovated apartment block where Alexis Michaels lived now. She'd pretty much given him the brush-off the last time he'd seen her. Funny, he mused, how people used the word *see* all the time, like "Nice to see you… you see what I mean."

At first Alexis had been distraught over losing her

sight. She'd fought her way back to health and sanity, helping him as best she could to find the bastard who'd attacked her, only to have him slip through their fingers.

Somehow, Alexis really got to him—really moved him. He'd once feared he'd left the soft side of himself back in the service, where he'd seen innocents maimed and killed. But Alexis had made him feel things again.

Blair realized he was half a block from the apartment he and his buddy Jace had helped Alexis move into last year. He popped a breath mint in his mouth in case he had dragon's breath after that sandwich. He'd just stop by for a sec to see how she was doing. Twice she'd turned him down for dinner, but he still couldn't get her out of his head.

As far as Blair could tell, Alexis had the smallest apartment in the rehabbed building. At least it was on the first floor, so she had only three stairs to deal with.

He went into the dim, narrow hall that led to the three first-floor apartments. Good, her mailbox and door did not bear her name. Voices sounded within. It would be great if she'd made new friends, since she'd distanced herself from her former acquaintances so that sicko Dortman couldn't trace her.

Squaring his shoulders, Blair knocked. The voices stopped; maybe she'd had the radio on.

"Who is it?" she asked through the door.

"Blair Ryan, Alexis. I was just in the area and thought I'd see how you're doing."

He heard her unlock the dead bolt, fumble with a safety chain, then turn the lock in the door handle. He'd installed the dead bolt for her the day he and Jace had moved her in here. He was relieved she used the safety measures even during the day, but then light and dark were the same to her. To his surprise, when the door opened, she stood bathed in sunlight from her front windows. With a little smile, she stuck out her hand.

He took it and shook it, then covered it with his other one for a second until she pulled gently away. She looked really good. Her jet-black hair was shorter, but it framed her lively face with gentle curls. He was glad she didn't have on the dark sunglasses she'd insisted on wearing after she was released from the hospital. Ironically, the appearance of her snappy, brown eyes had not been damaged, and she still turned them in the direction of speakers or noise.

The cuts and bruises on her forehead that had taken so long to turn to pale scars were hidden beneath wispy bangs. She was a natural beauty who didn't need makeup, with her dark, arched brows and thick eyelashes. She'd always looked pale, but now color suffused her cheeks and throat above the aqua, peasant-type blouse she wore with jeans. She was barefoot, and damn if she didn't have her toenails painted. He felt a bit guilty looking her over so thoroughly, something he would not have done if she could see him.

"Can you come in for a minute?" she asked. "I have something to tell you."

"Sure—not about Dortman?"

"No, thank heavens. I'm glad the coward's long gone, except that he might be harming someone else. Do you want to sit down?" she asked, gesturing toward the couch under the windows. "I can get you some iced tea if you'd like—or I can make coffee. I remember you like it with no cream but two packets of sweetener."

That little detail touched him. He cleared his throat. "Iced tea would be fine. It's warm out for April."

"I know. I've been enjoying the sun pouring in the windows."

He sat and she walked gracefully toward the kitchen. If he hadn't known better, he'd think she could see.

"I thought I heard voices in here when I knocked," he called to her, looking around the room. Everything was neat and uncluttered. Orchid plants and African violets bloomed on the window ledge.

"One of my talking books," she said from the kitchen. "Actually, it was a travel book about walking tours in London. I'd love to go visit again someday, maybe make a tour of famous literary places. Do you get that feeling—wanderlust?"

Man, she was in a good mood compared with other times he'd seen her. He bit his lip, smiling at the way she'd phrased that question. It wasn't wanderlust that called to him when he was around Alexis Michaels.

"After my stint in the marines, I'm pretty content at the old age of thirty-one to settle down, and this part of New Jersey's still home."

She came back into the living room with two glasses of iced tea and handed him one—right where he could easily take it from her.

Though he knew she couldn't see him, her gaze met his, and she nodded. She searched for her beanbag chair with her foot, then curled into it, cradling her glass on her knees. With this woman, even when she was laid out in a hospital bed, newly blinded with that beautiful face all bandaged up, he'd felt she could see inside him. As badly hurt as she'd been, she'd always shown great concern for his feelings, and she'd never blamed him for not finding and arresting Dortman—though he'd sure blamed himself.

"What I wanted to tell you," she said, "is that I'm getting a guide dog in two days. I'll be gone for a month's training and then—hopefully—have much more freedom when I return. Sometimes, though I still have students in to teach, it's like—like being in prison. Which reminds me, the dog I will get was raised in prison before it was trained."

"I've heard of that program. Puppies in Prison?"

"Puppies Behind Bars—prison bars, not the kind you Irish cops like to check out when you're off duty."

He chuckled. "Alexis, that's great. It will give you a lot more confidence to come and go."

"I thought you might give me a lecture that I'll get out more where someone who knows Dortman—you know—someone might see me."

"All life's a risk," he said, taking a big swig from

his glass, then putting it down on the slate-top coffee table beside the sofa. He leaned toward her, elbows on his knees. "I've seen security soldiers and explosives experts work with dogs in the middle of minefields, and the department here uses bomb- and drug-sniffing dogs. I'm pretty sure some of our bomb sniffers are from the PBB program."

"I feel it's a big step, but I'm ready for it. And I just want you to know that I appreciate all you've done for me since my acci— Well, I know you always call it an attack."

"That it was. Listen, how about we do something to celebrate this big step you're taking?" He could have bitten his tongue once he blurted that out. Each time he'd tried to get personal with her, she'd backed off, but it was too late now. "And I want to meet your new partner when you get back, okay?"

"Sure—about meeting my dog. You know, when I told my old roommate about the dog on the phone, she said, 'You mean a blind dog?' Of course, she meant a dog for the blind, but I told her, 'I hope he's not blind because he's going to have to take the lead,' and we laughed and laughed."

He was thrilled to see a smile light her face, and

had to blink back tears. Lucky she couldn't see them, because she always seemed to think he pitied her when that wasn't the case. Not at all, and he hoped to hell she'd let him prove it.

"About the celebration, Blair, I've got a student coming here in about an hour—she's preparing for college entrance exams she has to retake to get her scores up."

"Then how about a walk right now, even if it's just once around the block? Like you said, the sun's great today, spring has sprung and all that. I'm not as good as a guide dog, but we'll be just a couple of friends out for a short stroll, okay?"

He watched her grip her glass. She was going to turn him down again, and if she did, then that was that. He'd just phone her someday to ask how she was doing with her canine partner.

"I know it's always bothered you that Dortman took off before you could nail him," she said, "but I owe you so much, including letting me get iced tea for you without asking if you can help or doing it for me, like my mother and my friends always do."

"I'm not here because I feel guilty about Dortman, Alexis, and I'm not here to make sure you're keeping your door chain on or your new phone number unlisted. But if you don't have the time…"

"But I do," she said, getting up. "A walk outside sounds great. I've never had a dog, Blair. Can you tell me more about the ones you've seen people working with?"

He was so excited he felt like a kid again. She got her shoes and jacket, and though he wanted to help her into it, he let her do it alone. But he did take her hand and put it in the crook of his arm as they stepped outside together.

On her third day at the Independence Guide Dog School, Alexis was more keyed up than ever. After three days of general orientation and basic instruction about working with a guide dog, the students would meet their dogs today.

"Now, just let me review a few things," their instructor, Andy Curtis, told them in their classroom. "You've all come a long way since you arrived, but today you need to begin to bond with your partners before we can go on to make the two of you a great working pair. But keep in mind, even after this month of intensive training, you have not arrived. Training's an ongoing, lifelong thing with these dogs. It can take up to six months or more to become a good team. And, remember, the dogs are not only going to be your work companions when in harness, but your pets when they are out of harness. Today, you begin to build on that lifetime relationship with these dogs—their working lifetime, at least."

It sounded like a marriage, Alexis thought, a good one. But she was still nervous about making a commitment to a dog. Sure, she was ready to meet her partner, and she trusted the great job the staff at the school had done to prepare her, yet she was still scared.

So far this week, she had been surprised to learn how much work was required to exercise and groom a dog. Why, cats pretty much groomed themselves. And the dog would need periodic awards and praise for things well done, unlike cats, who were quite independent. But this had to work; she just had to bond with this dog. She knew her dog would be female— they all were—and she'd asked Andy if the partnerships sometimes didn't work out. He'd shaken his head and said, "It rarely happens." That worried her, too.

In the coming weeks, one trainer would work with six students. Quickly, Alexis reviewed the commands the dogs would already know: *sit, stand, stay, heel, forward, backward, steady* and *hup up,* meaning to speed up. Other commands would be optional, depending on the needs of the dog owner.

When Andy dismissed them, the students went to their private rooms down a long hall to await delivery of their dogs, which had been carefully matched with their new owners for size, strength and speed. Alexis had held on to a metal and leather harness connected to her instructor, then to a "demo-dog," so she could get the feel of it, all the while being observed for her pace and stride. She had also answered numerous questions about the area where she lived, her activities and lifestyle. She'd admitted she had felt like a recluse but was hoping the dog would help her get her freedom back. All she'd been told was that her dog was a twenty-two-inch-high, sixty-pound chocolate Labrador retriever named Sterling.

Alexis now sat on the floor with her back against her small bed in the room where so many other blind people must have waited to meet their dogs. Andy had suggested sitting on the floor because the dogs had learned not to leap up on furniture, and their initial exuberance could knock someone over. Her heart was pounding as hard as it did whenever Blair Ryan showed up in her life.

Alexis thought about all the help and support Blair had given her, even during the short walk they'd taken just five days ago. "Tree growing in the sidewalk at ten o'clock," he'd said as he'd steered her around the block. "Rough concrete coming, we're going to turn right in about four more steps." In a way, she thought, she would use the same sort of verbal commands and the dog's physical moves to help her maneuver.

She jumped at a knock on the door—no, it must be the one next door. The dogs were here.

Alexis felt bad that some of the people in her class had been blind from birth and would never really know what a Labrador retriever looked like. She felt blessed she'd seen Labs—yellow, black and chocolate—and knew how regal, how alert they were with those big, kind eyes. Chocolate for a color sounded warm and safe. Chocolate was also her favorite comfort food, and surely this dog would be a comfort.

Another knock, louder. She gripped her hands together in her lap. Yes, it was her door. She heard it open and felt the cooler breeze from the hall, then heard the dog's toenails on the tile floor.

"Alexis, here's your new partner, Sterling," Andy said. "And she's very excited to meet you."

That was all. She heard Andy drop the leash, then close the door. A solid, warm body covered in sleek fur pressed against her and a wet tongue licked her chin. Two big paws rested on her shoulders. Sterling's collar jingled; she was panting, and her tail *thump-thumped* against Alexis's knees.

Alexis patted her head and stroked her strong back and her muscular neck. She scratched Sterling behind her ears and, finally, found her voice.

"Sterling, Sterling, good girl, good girl! We're going to be best friends, work together, walk outside together…"

That was all she could manage before she hugged Sterling hard.

With their puppies under the table at their feet in the noisy, crowded prison cafeteria, the Puppies Behind Bars trainers sat down to eat lunch at the same table. Corky nestled tight against her legs, which Tina liked, though it was best that the puppies eventually learned to lie quietly and patiently, not touching legs or feet while their human partners sat at the table.

At first there was little chatter but the usual complaints about the food, which was downed fast enough. Tina kept her eyes on her plate because they were still red and swollen. She'd been a real wreck since the day of Mama's funeral. It was probably harder *not* being there than if she could have gone. The prison rules allowed her to go, but the expense for a guard would have come from Tina's family, and she was too worried there wasn't even enough money for a proper funeral. Besides, if she'd seen her kids, she could never have left them again. She was scared she'd have done something screwy and gotten herself even more time in here. Thinking about her little Larry and Sandy staying with strangers was even worse. Showing emotions in here was a sign of weakness, but since she'd started in the PBB program, she felt she could at least let loose a little with this bunch of inmates without being ridiculed or preyed upon. The puppies kind of softened everybody up.

"Man, that's really something, us teaching these dogs foreign phrases," Shawanna said. Like Tina, she was a veteran of the previous PBB program. She too had trained a guide dog last time. "Only foreign language I ever spoke was lotsa cursing and street slang. It's really neat to feel trusted. One year you're on the level with pond scum and the next you're helping out blind folks or preparing dogs to find explosives to save lives."

"I'd hate to think about Corky leaving the country, though," Tina put in. "But there's so much need here for EDCs that odds are our dogs will probably be somewhere nearby."

"I heard dogs have over a hundred million sniffing cells while people only have about five million," Lou Ann put in from farther down the table. She was new to the program, but it seemed to be helping her a lot already. She was pretty smart but had got in trouble for her big mouth at first. Still, being part of a team effort had made other people more tolerant of her.

"But I have to tell you, Tina," she went on, "some of the dogs so far have ended up working with cops in South Africa, Italy and the Far East. Hell, that's places I'll never see. PBB dogs worked at the pope's funeral and the Democratic and Republican national conventions. And one screens the mayor of New York's jet, as well as planes at the big airports."

"Wow, talk about that old telephone company ad, 'Reach out and touch someone,'" Karla mumbled, her mouth full. Karla had been over two hundred pounds when she first got here, but she'd been dropping some weight since she'd started exercising with her puppy, Brady.

Tina moved her foot closer to Corky's warmth. Even if she could get past mourning Mama and worrying about her kids, she'd still be worried about giving up Corky to a world of danger.

"Pretty funny, huh?" Shawanna said. "Here I was doing my best a coupla years ago to outsmart the cops, and now we're helping them outsmart the bad guys."

Panicked, his heart thudding, Blair Ryan sat straight up in bed. His sheet and blanket were wrapped like tight bandages around him. It was pitch-black. For a minute he couldn't recall where he was. He'd been falling, tumbling into blackness... Kabul? Hiding from the Taliban in the mountains? No, no, he was in his apartment at home.

Sweating, he strained to listen. Maybe a car had backfired to wake him. Or else he'd been dreaming about tank or gunfire.

Blair put his head in his hands. Please, dear God, not memories of those days. He'd never get back to sleep tonight. Jagged pieces of those nightmares floated through his sleep-sodden brain.

Or was he dreaming about Alexis, about what happened to her? He'd reached her right after the emergency squad did—seeing her crumpled like a doll at the bottom of the steps. Had Dortman been hiding there in the dark somewhere, watching, enjoying what he'd done?

Bits of the dream he'd just awakened from came back to him. Alexis had died. She was holding his hand, telling him that she needed a dog to be able to run away from cancer, but now it was too late. When he'd held her hand, her hair had turned lighter, and her face became Kate's.

He muttered an oath, ripped off the cocoon of covers and got out of bed. He hadn't dreamed of losing his sister for the longest time. She'd been eight years younger than him, and he'd felt he was her protector as well as her big brother. Although he knew you couldn't fight cancer with fists or even guns, he sometimes felt he'd failed her. How he'd love it if Kate were around. He could teach her things, show her things. He'd like her to meet Alexis.

He padded to the window and peered through the vertical blinds. His bedroom overlooked carports and more apartments. The late-April moon was half-full, throwing gray shadows. Was Len Dortman out there somewhere, harming other women, as Alexis feared? Did he know what he'd done to the woman he'd been obsessed with, or did he think he'd killed her and fled a murder charge? It wasn't the M.O. of an obsessive-compulsive like that to just move on.

Blair shook his head to clear it. Though he was still sweating, he felt chilled. Standing at the window, legs spread, his fists thrust under his armpits, he wished he could hold Alexis in the moonlight, in the sunlight, anytime or place—protect her and yet help her regain her independence. He hoped Dortman was gone for good, although a part of him couldn't help but wish he could get his hands on the guy—just once.

CHAPTER
~ THREE ~

With Sterling guiding her, Alexis walked with grace and confidence again, not afraid to stride out, not fearful that she'd take a tumble over some object she couldn't see. The dog had even pulled her back from a pothole in the street—at least that's what Andy had called out to her to explain Sterling's sudden detour.

She held the leash between the index and middle fingers of her right hand and the harness handle with her left. At first it had felt strange to trust her movements to an animal, but after a week of practice she felt as if she had wings—or at least steady feet again.

"Don't let her set the pace, Alexis!" Andy called from behind her. "Remember, you're the alpha dog here, not her."

Alexis nodded and smiled. In one of the classes, they'd discussed dog psychology. Dogs were inherently pack animals and needed to know where they came in the pecking order of power, so to speak. She'd been surprised to learn that a dog as beautifully mannered and trained as Sterling would test whoever was in charge, but the two of them struck a better balance every day. And, though dealing with a dog for the first time in her life had taken getting used to, she already appreciated and admired Sterling.

The Lab led her into the obstacle course that was the adventure of the day, as the students called these excursions. Yesterday they had walked down a busy street and tomorrow would begin practice in crossing streets. The students and their dogs had worked this course, which was set up in part of a parking lot, earlier in the week, but the obstacles had been rearranged.

And that made Alexis realize that trying to fix the pattern of the barriers in her mind had been foolish. That, and banging her shins into what felt like a tall, plastic garbage can.

"Ow!" she cried, inadvertently jerking on Sterling's leash. "It's okay, good dog," she added quickly. After all, the dog had tried to lead her around the obstacle.

"Alexis," Andy called out, "the point is to trust your seeing partner. Did you feel Sterling try to take you farther left to avoid that garbage can?"

"Yes," she admitted. "Mea culpa. I guess I was trying to guide her."

"Trust, trust and more trust," he said, his voice coming closer as he approached. "Let Sterling make those key decisions. It's what she's been trained to do—wants to do."

"Right. Sorry." Alexis knew she needed Andy's help, but it was making her nervous that he kept following them, watching them. It reminded her of the way she'd felt those weeks Len Dortman trailed her—both the times she knew he was watching her and the times she only feared he was. But she was not going to let that get to her, absolutely not.

"Go ahead, Alexis," Andy encouraged her. "As my high-school football coach used to tell us, the most important play is the next play, not the one where you just fumbled. These dogs have been taught 'intelligent disobedience,' remember?"

She did remember. Guide dogs were taught to obey commands unless they saw a problem or danger, such as an approaching car that their partner did not hear. Even if the dog had been told "forward," the animal would disobey if she sensed or saw a threat.

"Forward, Sterling. Good girl, forward."

Alexis allowed the dog more leeway now, walking with her, not fighting her, trying to feel her moves through the harness. Ha, like dancing with a partner who knew how to lead, she thought, then thrust from her mind the memory of Blair asking her to dinner and dancing. She had to focus on this and not let her thoughts wander. Sterling was concentrating, and she must, too.

But the dog seemed to have led her into a dead end. Sterling stopped and turned them both one hundred eighty degrees around in a small space.

"Is this a maze?" Alexis called to Andy.

"Only if you don't follow your partner's lead. And this might be a good time to decide if you want to teach Sterling the additional command of 'find the way,'" he suggested, coming closer again. "It's different from 'forward.' When you're in a tight or crowded place without a straight-ahead path or exit, it's a useful command—up to you."

Alexis nodded. "I have a very smart partner here. Yes, I'll teach her that. Especially because I believe that I—we—are in another dead end," she announced as the stalwart dog pivoted them again.

"Find the way, Sterling," Alexis commanded in the calm, clear voice she was learning to use with the Lab when she was working. She used softer tones when Sterling was out of harness, when she played with her or groomed her, or when they just relaxed together. "Find the way."

And Sterling did.

Tina lifted an armful of soiled prison uniforms into the big washer, set the controls and turned it on. Nothing happened. But it had just been working a minute ago.

Then she saw she had not completely closed the door. She slammed it, automatically glancing down to where Corky should be. But this was the weekend the puppies were gone to host families on the outside, a part of the program that happened as often as twice a week. All of the prisons raising dogs for the blind offered "Puppies by the Hour" to outsiders who wished to puppy-sit and play with the dogs. This helped to socialize the dogs, letting them ride in a car, live in a house, be around kids.

Kids...

Tina sniffed and blew her nose before she went back to sorting piles of dirty towels. Besides missing her kids so bad, she was still mourning Mama. Whether she wanted the memories or not, scenes from her childhood had been rotating through her mind like the clothes going around in the washer...

Happy times, mostly. There'd been a bad fallout when she'd married Hank. Mama had seen he was rotten to the core even then, but Tina had had to find out the hard way. "You oughta be more like your sister Vanessa, trying to make something of herself!" Mama had scolded. But Vanessa took off and didn't look back. Still, Tina was sure Vanessa would be heartbroken if she knew Mama had passed on and her sister's kids were more or less orphans.

Tina had also been real antsy waiting to hear whether her kids were going to be placed in foster homes or stay with children's services in the city. She was torn about that. She'd like them to have a family, but what if they then realized what losers their own parents were? What if Larry and Sandy decided they hated her when each day she knew just how much she loved them and how badly she'd hurt—damaged them.

She threw a ripped-up towel in the recycle bin, then leaned her elbows on the counter and propped up her head with her hands. But she looked up as a new inmate, Lupe, noisily rolled another huge hamper of soiled uniforms into the steamy room.

"You miss-eeng that leetle dog again, *sí?*"

Tina nodded and went back to sorting. Lupe's English had been pretty bad when she'd come in here, but she'd been trying to improve. She said she might as well learn something worthwhile in here.

That's the way Tina looked at the PBB program— learning something useful while she was in prison. The fact she took such pride in caring for her dogs made her think she might try to open a dog-sitting or grooming business when she got out. Not that people would trust an ex-con to dog-sit in their homes, not that she'd ever be able to afford a shop of her own, but surely someone would hire her. Her dream was to own a van and go house to house, working right in the van—dog groomer on call.

Tina sighed. Could she make enough doing that to support her kids, make things up to them? Could—

She looked up and saw Ellen enter the laundry-room door and head straight for her. Tina twisted the towel she held, feeling as edgy as if she'd been caught shoplifting.

"Tina, some good news," the officer told her, glancing down at the notebook she carried. "The warden would have told you herself, she said, but she's in a parole board hearing and thought you should know this right away. Your little girl's been taken by a foster family, people who live in the country and have two other kids and a dog for her to play with. Bet that cheers you up!"

"But—not my boy? Larry's not with her?"

Ellen frowned down at her notebook. "No—I— nothing about him, just your girl."

"I was hoping, praying they wouldn't be pulled apart. They need each other—that's all they have left right now."

Oh, damn, Tina thought, she was going to cry again. And Corky wasn't here to help.

Blair Ryan waited until two days after Alexis said she'd be home before calling her. He didn't want her to think he was overanxious to see her—which he was. Then too, he'd been working a tough domestic-violence case where the husband, despite a restraining order, had returned to the home and assaulted his estranged wife really badly. They'd caught and arrested the guy. The situation wasn't that close to Alexis's, and yet her case returned to haunt him again.

He leaned back in his desk chair and reached over piles of files and reports for the phone. The buzz of business could be heard outside his cubicle.

He punched in redial. Again, Alexis's home phone rang. For the second time today—and it was only mid-morning—his own voice came on with, "If you wish to leave a message…" The day she'd moved into her new place, he'd suggested that he record the answering machine message for her so that a caller who didn't know her—or was looking for her—would think a man was on the premises. It had gone unspoken between them that, even though the number would be unlisted, someone as devious as Dortman could find it.

Not wanting her to worry about a call where the person just hung up—that had been one of Dortman's tricks before things escalated—Blair said, "Alexis,

Blair again. I'll bet you're out with your new guide dog. Call me if you get a chance, because I'd like to meet him or her. I'm at my work number, but I told you that you can always phone me at home, and my cell number's the same. Hope to see you—hear from you."

He hung up, wishing he hadn't sounded so forlorn. But he missed her. Man, get a life, he told himself as he hunched back over his desk and fingered through the folder he kept on Len Dortman. Blair was over-burdened with work and should have filed it by now. In a way, he was hoping it would turn into a cold case that would never be needed again. But the guy's psychological workup indicated his single-mindedness, and that scared Blair.

He skimmed Dortman's psychological profile. The perp's mother had deserted him as a child, and he'd evidently had violent reactions to rejection or separation from women because of major self-esteem issues. The guy wasn't that bad-looking, and came off as Mr. Nice-and-Helpful at first, so it could be possible he'd find a victim who needed him—though she'd be in real danger if she acted even slightly in-dependent, let alone tried to get rid of him.

* * *

As she and Sterling walked from the apartment to a small, neighborhood grocery store, Alexis was thrilled to realize what a difference this dog had made in her life already. Holding on to the harness and trusting the dog, she was no longer afraid of taking a walk or going on an errand.

Besides, a guide dog was a real attraction. People she didn't know talked to her and Sterling, though if they edged too close and she thought they might pet Sterling, she explained that it was best not to touch a guide dog when she was working. "She's gentle as can be," she'd tell people, "but when she's in the harness, she leaves her pet status behind to become my guide and protector."

Even strangers said things like, "Wow, I can tell your dog's real smart!"

"She sure is," Alexis would tell them. "Sterling is smart and well trained—she totally impresses me!"

But when they were walking, Alexis had to concentrate. No strolling along just daydreaming. She had her cell phone with her in case she needed to make a call, but she didn't turn it on because she didn't want that distraction either. Alexis had to make key decisions about where they were going and when they'd arrived. It was indeed a working partnership, and she cherished Sterling for giving her some semblance of the independence she'd had before disaster struck.

When Sterling was out of harness, she became a lively, loving pet, and Alexis knew the dog's big, warm body well now from playing and hugging: the distinctive tail, thick at the base and tapering toward the tip; the short, dense coat and powerful jaws, which were so gentle. She lavished affection on Sterling—even scratching the dog's belly when she rolled on her back.

Alexis knew she'd never responded to an independent, sometimes aloof cat this way. It didn't even startle her now when Sterling licked her face, and she talked to her so much more than she did to Chaucer. The cat got along with the dog quite well, since Sterling stuck to the floor and stayed off the sofa and window ledges where Chaucer perched among the potted plants.

The only thing that still bothered Alexis was crossing busy streets, and there were plenty of those around here. Not being able to tell if the traffic light was in their favor or not, the dog stopped at the curb. It was up to Alexis to listen for vehicular and pedestrian traffic before giving Sterling the forward command. But the dog then looked to be sure it was safe. If Sterling saw something Alexis hadn't discerned, she might refuse to cross or even pull her firmly back from danger. If only she'd had a protector like this when her life had turned into such a nightmare.

This time Sterling didn't budge when Alexis gave the forward command. "Good girl, Sterling," Alexis told her as a cyclist turned a corner so close she could hear the pedals moving the chain and feel the push of wind as the rider sped by. "Forward, Sterling." When it was all clear, the dog took her across the street.

Some observers were certain Sterling was reading the traffic lights. A man had said to them yesterday, "Hey, lady, I thought dogs were color-blind. Do they teach them that the one on top is the green light?"

Alexis had to bite her lip not to laugh at that one. Yes, both she and Sterling had to make decisions, but they got around, farther and better each of the days she was back home. She couldn't wait to show her mother what a change this had made in her life. And she wanted Blair to see. That way if he still kept coming around, she'd be sure it wasn't out of guilt or pity.

The next day, Blair sat at a table outside the Tapitias, a café-restaurant about six blocks from Alexis's place, waiting for her. "I'll be the one with a dog," she'd told him with a little laugh when she'd returned his call. She'd sounded lighthearted and confident. No tremor in her voice, no hesitation. His hopes soared.

And now, here she came, striding along at a good clip, her hair blowing, her lips moving. Evidently she was talking to the dog. Sterling was a brown beauty, and Blair's eyes stung with unshed tears. He and Kate had owned a Labrador like that, only black instead of this chocolate color.

He stood at the table he'd taken for them. He wasn't sure whether to call to her or approach her. There was a low, plastic barrier around these tables, but she'd chosen the place, so she must know it well. As she came closer, he saw the dog hesitate a moment at the barrier, which reached its nose.

"Forward," he heard Alexis say. Then she must have felt the barrier, because she added, "Find the way, Sterling, find the way." At that, the dog took her around to the entry.

Alexis could feel Blair's presence before she heard him say, "Alexis! I'm over here, coming your way."

She smiled in the direction of his voice. He must have been watching for her. Strange how she was developing a sort of sixth sense when someone was studying her, not just passing by. She wasn't sure if it was because she'd spent three weeks being watched by her instructor, or whether she just knew that more people were watching her now, the blind woman and her smart dog. Despite the warm day, she shivered. If someone stalked her now, would she sense his presence, separate from those who had no intention of harming her?

She prayed she wasn't slipping back into the paranoia and trauma of the days when Dortman stalked her. No, it couldn't be that. She'd been so oblivious to him at first, but once she'd spotted him, he seemed to be everywhere, following her on the street, in his car, watching her front door, skulking behind every darn tree!

"Blair!" she said, recognizing his familiar quick

stride. She heard him stop right in front of her. "As you can see I've got my hands full or I'd shake your hand," she added with a smile. "Let's sit down."

"Sure, I have a table—right over here. This way," he added.

But she just said, "Forward, Sterling," and moved in his direction with the dog.

The minute she dropped the leash and harness, the Lab lay down under their table, quiet and patient, while Blair helped to seat her. "That's one beautiful animal," he said. "I'll bet she enjoys roughhousing."

"She's beautifully behaved indoors and out, but yes, she loves to play."

A moment's silence hung between them while life bustled all around—voices, car horns, even the song of a robin as the city edged from winter into spring.

"It's working out great, isn't it?" he asked.

"Better than I could have hoped. She's given me back my legs and my life, at least this version of it. It's taken some getting used to, being so responsible for her well-being, too, but I owe her so much."

Their server came. They ordered fajitas and sangria. The dog didn't budge.

"Nothing for Sterling while she's working, right?" Blair asked.

"If it's a hot day, I take water along, but that's it. Would you believe it—a dog that doesn't stop to sniff at things or beg for food when she's out? You could put a piece of prime rib in front of her, and she wouldn't take it when she's in harness. She's my gentle giant."

"That reminds me—I checked and learned that the same program Sterling came from has supplied several of our police department's bomb-sniffing dogs. Those EDC dogs need to be calm and obedient and want to please their owners—handlers, in this case. The love and care they're given as puppies also prepares them to handle the later extensive scent-association training. They're far different from the attack-on-command police dogs, though people sometimes get that confused."

After they ate, they walked together toward a small park behind the local elementary school. A jumble of kids' voices filled the air. Blair told her that Latino kids were playing soccer in a field next to a baseball diamond where Indian students were enjoying a game of cricket. This park was an arm of the big city park where Alexis had been jogging the night Dortman attacked her, the night she fell—or was thrown—down the concrete steps by the old amphitheater.

She took Sterling's harness off and let her run a bit. She and Blair took turns throwing a small, foam football, which the dog retrieved, faithfully dropping it at Alexis's feet, even when Blair had heaved it.

Blair didn't want to talk about his latest case, and all she wanted to talk about was Sterling, but their conversation eventually spun off to everyday topics like the weather and local politics, their favorite CDs and TV shows. He was amazed she was familiar with a popular new dance competition on TV.

"What?" she said, taking a little swipe at his shoulder and landing the blow. "There's a police department rule that blind people have to stick to radio or CDs instead of TV? I just listen to the music on the show and imagine what they're doing, then listen to the judges' evaluations. Sometimes I dance around myself, just for fun," she admitted. "Sterling watched every move I made the other night and thought I did really well. I believe she gave me a ten."

Alexis hadn't meant to say all that. It sounded like a come-on to get him to ask her to go dancing again.

She was about to change the subject when Blair blurted, "How about just for fun, I take you dancing? You said no before, but things are different now that you've cleared a big hurdle. Of course, Sterling would come, too, and sit like a guardian angel under the table."

Blair sounded breathless—just the way Alexis felt. He'd asked her to go to some retro place called Casablanca before, which played 1940s music and was really popular. She'd wondered if the place was decorated with blowup photos of Ingrid Bergman and Humphrey Bogart from the old black-and-white movie. What was that famous line the two endangered lovers said? Oh, yeah, "We'll always have Paris." But if she didn't at least accept his invitation this time, she'd never have memories of dancing—even in the dark.

"All right," she said, and thought she heard him exhale in relief. "If you and Sterling are game, so am I."

CHAPTER
~FOUR~

It turned out that the Club Casablanca was just on the other side of the big park from Alexis's neighborhood. The evening was so lovely and mild that she and Blair decided to walk. Alexis had to smile, and not just from happiness: it had been years since she'd had a chaperone when she went out on a date, and never one so welcome as Sterling.

And she'd never cared for anyone she'd been with as much as she cared for Blair Ryan. She'd admitted it to herself now, though the possibility of being more than friends still seemed as distant as sight and light.

"I know it's dark, but here I am picturing this walk as if it were daytime," she told Blair. He walked easily along on Sterling's other side, content to let the dog lead, satisfied not to talk too much so she could concentrate. Of course, with Blair, she could have left Sterling home, but after all, he'd invited the dog, too, and being in an atmosphere of music and movement would be good practice for her canine companion as well as for herself.

"The streetlights are on and, better yet, there's a moon," Blair told her. "It's almost full."

When they stopped at an intersection with a light, she asked, "Can you see the mountains and plains on the moon clearly tonight?"

"Pretty clear," he said.

"Remember Neil Armstrong's words when he first set foot on the moon? Something like 'One small step for man, one giant leap for mankind'? Well, working with Sterling has been one small step for this woman and yet one giant leap, too. Thank God for Puppies Behind Bars and that great guide dog school—and you, Blair."

"I hope you'll whisper something like that in my ear when we're dancing and not when we have

Sterling walking between us—and the light just turned green."

"Sterling, forward."

The club was noisy with chatter and music. A live band—Blair said six men—accompanied a male and a female singer and played golden oldies, great dance tunes from the 1930s and '40s. While Sterling lay quiet and content under their table, they danced to a tune made famous by Fred Astaire and Ginger Rogers, "I Won't Dance." But they were dancing, cheek to cheek, their arms around each other, moving closer together with each spin around the dance floor.

"I agonized about whether to keep calling you," he whispered as the live band switched to "In the Mood." "I didn't want to seem unprofessional, and I didn't want you to think that I was just upset I hadn't found Dortman."

"Don't say that name," she said, touching her forehead to his strong, square jaw. "I just want to forget about him."

He sighed so hard that his chest shifted up, then down, against her breasts. She felt that little touch clear down to the pit of her belly.

"I know, Alexis, but I've tried that with a personal tragedy, and it doesn't work. We lost my younger sister, Kate, to cancer when she was nine. When I try to forget about it, bury it, it comes out in nightmares and depression. I've hated hospitals ever since and tried to keep from really caring deeply for someone so I wouldn't be hurt again—that's nuts, I know."

"But I understand," she reassured him. "I didn't know about that—and you were so good to keep visiting me when I was in the hospital. Blair, I know it's far too late, and I didn't even know Kate, but I'm so sorry. When I was in the hospital, I got to know some people who've been blind since birth. I had so many sighted years and I'm still healthy—and alive, no thanks to Dortman. That makes me realize how blessed I am, especially now that I have Sterling. But I'll take your advice about not trying to shut the bad things out."

"That doesn't mean you let the bad past get in the way of the good future," he murmured and gave her waist a little squeeze as he spun her again.

"Blair, forward," she said with a little laugh. "Find the way."

"Yes, ma'am. But just remember, cops are very—

well, dogged—about following commands. I would like for us to find the way."

She smiled and clasped his neck and hand just a bit harder as they slowed again, standing almost in place, swaying with the music. Dancing with Blair, she could just close her eyes and move, feeling his lead, his strength—even his deep concern. And if that was love, could she trust it would be enough? Earlier, he'd said all good things were worth the risk.

She inhaled the clean, tart scent of his aftershave. He emanated warmth and security. Yet as safe as she felt with him, in his arms like this, she was also afraid of how much she wanted him. She wondered if she had spoken the thought out loud, because he tipped her chin up and covered her lips with his.

Instantly, she stopped moving, her mouth responding to his. They stumbled slightly, but he held her up, which broke the kiss. They laughed, and clasping his hand tightly, she let him lead her back to their table. She reached down to stroke Sterling's head as she sat.

"Let's get back," he said, his voice a rough whisper.

No, that wasn't Kenneth Branagh's voice, she thought, and not his face either, only Blair's. She wanted to see him with her fingertips and her lips. She wanted to know everything about him.

"All right. I'm ready."

He paid the server, and they downed the rest of their wine. The male singer began to croon a tune called "Begin the Beguine" as they made their way out of the club.

"Let's cut through the park," she said, surprised at her own request. "I do want to move beyond the past, and besides, there are some nice benches by the lake. The area still has lots of streetlights, doesn't it?"

"Sure, and people are walking there. Fine by me."

"Besides, Sterling deserves a little romp."

"Sterling? How about me?"

She laughed again, and they crossed the street, walking along the soft park grass to the gravel path, the one she'd been jogging on the night she was attacked. It hadn't been in this part of the park, though. Still, the amphitheater loomed between here and the area where she'd been running when Dortman must have appeared. She wished she could recall what had happened, but then again, maybe she didn't. She took off Sterling's harness, and Blair threw sticks for the dog to chase while they sat on a stone bench. The leaves were budding on the trees, and the wet soil of spring smelled fresh and fertile.

They held hands, then kissed. They made plans to go to the beach this summer, to have a picnic in the country—just the three of them. She said she'd like him to see her small hometown, and he even volunteered to meet her mother. It seemed, Alexis thought as she bent to put Sterling back into harness, her nightmares had turned to dreams.

In her cell that evening, after dinner, Tina reread the fax from her son Larry's caseworker for the fourth time. Even though she was incarcerated, children's services was trying to keep her informed, no matter how bad the news. The fax read:

We are endeavoring to place Lawrence Clawson in a stable, welcoming foster home. But most of our placements are currently of younger children or girls. So for the foreseeable future, until someone suitable is located and approved, Lawrence will remain in the custody of children's services. We regret that your children are not together, but circumstances dictate that—"

Tina threw the paper down and hit the mattress with her fist so hard that Corky jumped and looked up from her padded bed on the floor of the cell.

"Sorry, girl. It's all my fault. But, you know, I think if I'd had you and Sterling before I'd had my own two babies, I'd have been a better mom, and then this wouldn't all be happening."

"Hi, Tina," came a voice through the barred window of the steel door. Tina jerked her head around. It was Brenda, a floor officer, with Jeannie, their silver-haired Puppies Behind Bars instructor. Tina and Corky were due at a rare evening meeting in a little while, so she had to pull herself together. But why was Jeannie coming here?

This must mean more bad news. Tina felt her insides freeze over with fear.

"Ms. Lancer would like to have a little chat," Brenda said, unlocking the cell door.

Tina stood. Corky did, too, staring at the two intruders as if she was on guard. Then she evidently scented or recognized Jeannie and padded over to be petted. Everyone in the PBB program liked this woman, who was formerly a breeder of Labradors. Tina tried not to frown, but she felt herself stiffen.

"I'm just wondering how you and Corky are getting along," Jeannie said, bending to pat the puppy. "Since you had such success with Sterling, I thought maybe you could give me an honest appraisal. The thing is, I know you've been through some really tough times lately, and I just want to be sure you don't think your…depression…is affecting Corky's well-being."

Tina's stomach twisted. Were they going to take Corky away?

"I know Corky relies on me, but I rely on her, too," Tina blurted, then could have kicked herself. She didn't want to give Jeannie or anyone an opening to reassign her puppy. What if they thought she was too unstable to help raise Corky?

"Do you think that your needs sometimes get in the way of her concentrating on the task at hand—that is, what you're trying to teach her?" Jeannie asked.

"No, she can concentrate real good. I think the love I give her and the way we need each other—maybe even more right now than most inmates need their puppies—is good for her. After all, think how much her handler is going to have to rely on her to be strong to sniff out all kinds of explosives. The way I love Corky is a two-way street, and that's what a dog like this will need in the future—love and feedback for the good job she does."

"Tina, I just want the best for both of you," Jeannie said. "You proved what a fine job you can do with Sterling last time, so—"

"I'm working through my problems, and I can still change more. I changed a lot since I been serving my sentence here."

"What about your family situation right now?" Brenda asked.

"Yeah, my daughter's been placed in a foster home, and I just got a letter about trying to place my son, too…" Her voice trailed off. She retrieved the letter from her bed and held it up to them before she realized that in her frustration she'd twisted it like a licorice stick.

"I heard about your family, and I'm so sorry," Jeannie said.

"I appreciate that." Tina struggled to show these women she could keep calm. Were they putting her through this questioning to see if she would break? "I'm handling my tough times. Just like these puppies,

I'm learning patience. I've learned teamwork and self-control in this program, and I can teach that to Corky. I've seen how much having a routine and plans and responsibilities have helped the dogs and me. Give me more time with her—all the time she should have, and you'll see a dog as perfect as Sterling was."

As she spoke, Corky moved forward to stand beside her. Damn, but it was like the dog understood what was going on and was trying to help out. Didn't that count for something?

"Tina," Jeannie said, holding her hands up, palms out, "no dog—just like no person—is perfect. As gentle as Sterling was, you remember how she would sometimes growl when voices were raised. The guide dog instructor told me she was steady as a rock when walking by jackhammers blasting apart a sidewalk, yet when those women in the domestic-violence class cried or shouted, she reacted."

"But Sterling came through with flying colors, and Corky—and I—will, too," Tina insisted.

"Good enough." Jeannie gave a quick nod. "Then I'll see you and Corky in about—" she glanced at a large watch on her left wrist "—half an hour."

"For sure. We'll be there, ready to go."

Once she heard them walk away, Tina collapsed on the edge of her bed and leaned over to hug Corky. "Thanks for the help, girl," she whispered. "See how smart you are? You just sniffed out how bad I needed you to stand up with me."

"Do you want to come in for a few minutes?" Alexis asked Blair as he and Sterling brought her to her door after walking the rest of the way through the park, even past the amphitheater. Alexis had said it was like exorcising some demon, but she'd admitted she still could not recall exactly how she'd fallen down those steps.

"Sure," he said. "And I'll try to abide by your few minutes' curfew."

As she dug her keys out of her purse, Blair was tempted to take them from her to open the door, but he let her feel for the keyhole and put the key in herself.

"Home, Sterling," she said as she opened the door. "We're home."

"Is *home* one of the regular commands?" Blair asked as he followed her in and closed and locked the door behind them. She snapped on the light over her small dining area, then removed Sterling's leash. The Lab shook herself once as if to say, "That's a good night's work done," then plopped on her padded dog bed along the far wall.

"No, but I've been slowly adding commands like that and f-i-n-d t-h-e w-a-y," Alexis said, spelling the words as if Sterling were a kid. "Make yourself at home. Can I get you anything?"

"Just get yourself over here so we can continue what we started in the park."

It thrilled him that she simply dropped her purse on the table and strode to the couch. It was a deep, soft sofa with bolsters along the back, which made it hard to sit erect. He reached for her hand and tugged her down beside him. Their weight rolled them into the pillows so they were half sitting, half lying back.

"Blair, could I feel your face? To—to see you as best I can?"

In answer, he guided her right hand upward so her palm and fingers touched his left cheek. She'd known how smooth his skin was from dancing so close, though now she felt the slightest hint of stubble. No mustache; very short sideburns. She felt the angular line of his jaw and high cheekbones, too. Gently, she

300

ran her fingertips along his temple, through the crisp, short hair on both sides of his broad forehead, then back where it became thicker and longer. She had wondered if his haircut would be marine-short or artsy long, but it was in between.

"I grew it out from the jarhead look I used to have," he whispered as if he'd read her mind.

"Shh!"

She ran her fingers along his thick, sleek eyebrows and down the strong bridge of his nose. It was just slightly crooked with a bump. "A broken nose from when you were a kid?" she asked.

"An arrest gone wrong. But I thought I was supposed to keep quiet."

Ignoring his teasing, Alexis felt where his nostrils flared, felt his warm breath coming quickly. She touched his thick eyelashes and then his lips. Straight, taut lips, but the bottom one slightly pouted—poised for another kiss perhaps? He did kiss her fingertips, then nibbled at them.

"If you don't know how my lips feel by now," he said, "we have a lot of work to do."

He pulled her to him so she was sprawled across his lap and kissed her once, twice. They breathed in unison, their breath coming more quickly with each kiss. Perhaps, now, Alexis thought, she had really found the way.

Blair left shortly after——and it was a good thing, because he was showing more self-control than she was. Alexis was so excited she couldn't sleep. Was the impact of kissing magnified when someone was blind? If so, making love with Blair would send her off the charts.

And, she thought, trying to make herself settle down to earth, she and Blair Ryan seemed meant for each other. After all, he'd kept coming back even after the way she'd treated him at first. And she knew she could trust him. A man who was willing to drive to a tiny town two hours away on his day off to meet her mother had to be sincere. She'd been so wrong to let what had happened to her make her fear men.

"Sterling, my girl," she told the dog, "we are going to celebrate. I'm getting you an extra treat and a bath."

Sterling knew what *treat* meant. The word seemed to be branded on her canine heart. In the kitchen, she gobbled up the milk-bone snack, then marched right into the bathroom with Alexis while she filled the tub and got the doggie shampoo and three big towels. She made sure the water was the right temperature, because Sterling was anxious, bumping and nuzzling her.

"All right, in you go," Alexis said, and the dog got in as if she knew all those words, too. The running water made a lot of noise, but she thought she heard—or sensed—a knock on the front door. "Sterling, stay. Sit."

Could Blair have come back and be knocking? In the hall, at the door to the bathroom, she strained to listen.

No, nothing. But there did seem to be a cool draft from the back of the apartment.

Behind her, Sterling started to whine and slosh around in the water.

"Blair?" Alexis called.

A hall floorboard creaked in the direction of her bedroom.

"Lover boy's gone," said a voice she knew all too well. She gasped and stepped back against the bathroom door frame. "But don't be sad, 'cause you got me, babe—this time for good."

CHAPTER
❧ FIVE ❧

This was a nightmare! Alexis thought. She had to be dreaming.

But she knew she wasn't.

Len Dortman's voice was just as she'd remembered. The apartment felt heavy with his presence.

Her first instinct was to scream—to run for the front door, but she'd take too long with the locks. She could try to get to her purse on the table and her cell phone so she could call Blair, call 911. Or turn off the lights so Dortman couldn't see, then run to the front window, break the glass and scream. He must have come in the back. Did he jimmy open a window, one she could use to escape?

Her brain processed all her options in a split second of disbelief and horror. His footsteps came closer. He slammed the bathroom door, evidently to keep Sterling in, and grabbed her arm, then half heaved, half spun her into the living room and onto the couch. She felt her robe split open; she wore only a sleep shirt under it.

She righted herself fast, but he slammed down beside her, pulling her to him. His fist clenched her hair to hold her still, inches from his face; she smelled him and his clothes—sweat, liquor, tobacco.

And then she knew she'd have to find much more courage than she'd ever had in her life. More than she'd needed to face blindness or risk trusting—and loving—Blair. *Blair!* she tried to send him a mental message. *He's back, he's here. Come save me!*

But she knew she'd have to save herself. One of her neighbors was away this weekend, and the other was a hard-of-hearing old lady, so screaming might not work.

She chose not to fight—not yet at least. *Stay! Sit!* She gave herself Sterling's commands and willed herself to be as steady as her dog.

"Long time no see, Alexis," Dortman held her

upper arms in a brutal grip. She almost gagged as she inhaled his breath.

Did he know that she was blind? She wasn't sure, but she could think of no way to fool him on that. She braced herself to remember all that she and Blair had discussed about this monster. Don't anger him, she told herself. Don't let him think you're rejecting him.

"You do know I can't see anymore?" Her voice was quavering. She spoke up to make herself sound less afraid. "That night you left me hurt at the bottom of the steps, I lost my sight."

"I read it online from the *Star Ledger*."

She had to keep him talking.

"You're the one who ran," he said, his voice accusing. "I only meant to grab you—hold you—at the top of the steps, but you fell down backward. It wasn't my fault."

"I realize that now. I'm not blaming you. Actually, I could hardly recall what happened that night—head injury."

"What happened is that I stopped you on the path and told you how things had to be between us—what a mistake you'd made to get me fired."

"I didn't intend that. It's just that I expect someone who cares for me to give me some space if I ask for it."

"Space!" he roared, shaking her. "You wanted me out of your way, out of your life!"

"No, your—your intensity just scared me, that's all."

"If you want a wimp, you're not the woman I thought. I could tell you wanted me, too, so why did you have to play hard to get?"

"I just wasn't ready for such a commitment then. But now that I've had a lot of time to think things over, I'm not so sure."

"Blindness taught you that—or missing me?"

"It's hard to say. I'm still working it all through, and I just need a little more time from you."

He snorted. "*Away* from me, you mean."

But she was grateful to feel him ease his grip on her arms a bit. She heard Sterling pacing in the bathroom. Guide dogs were bred to calmly, gently accept new people, so what good would it do her to have Sterling in here? Whatever happened to her, she couldn't bear to have that beautiful dog hurt, too.

"The thing I want to know," he said, giving her

another little shake, "is that if you agree it wasn't my fault, then why were the cops on my back?"

"Of course it wasn't your fault, especially since you say I just fell. I guess the police have to investigate everything, that's all. I had weeks in the hospital to think things over——and then to be blind and need someone to help me." The words almost burned her mouth to say them. "I remember how much you wanted to be with me... Well, that's one reason I had to get a guide dog. I need someone with me all the time to lead me around. And I realized too late how loyal you were to me, how much you tried to care for me."

"You're lying. I seen Mr. Twinkle Toes dancing with you tonight—and you invited him in."

He'd been watching her and Blair. And if he knew Blair was the one who'd been hunting him...

"How long have you been back in town?" she asked, stalling for time, praying she could reach something to hit him with.

"Long enough to see you necking in the park with that guy, and who knows what else. I mighta been content to just keep watching you and the dog for a while, but what I saw tonight made me realize I got to get you away from him, one way or the other."

* * *

Blair couldn't sleep. He kept pacing back and forth from his kitchenette to his front door in the dark. Everything seemed to be going his way, but he still couldn't sleep. His mind was going a mile a minute, and he was on his third peanut-butter-and-jelly sandwich and glass of milk, even though he and Alexis had enjoyed dinner earlier. Talk about women being stress eaters!

He was certain that he wanted to marry Alexis Michaels. Sure, there would be risks and challenges, but that was true of many marriages. Yeah, there would be things they'd never be able to do together because she was visually impaired. It would mean always having a guide dog with them, though he'd rather be in the company of Sterling than many humans he'd known. Rearing kids someday would be a huge challenge for Alexis.

He knew he was rushing things—probably rushing her—but he couldn't help it. Not that he was going to show up on her doorstep tomorrow morning on bended knee, holding out a diamond engagement ring, but he wanted to level with her soon. He wanted to build on the trust they'd started to share.

He didn't like or want any surprises when he told her he loved her and wanted to spend his life with her—and Sterling—and live happily ever after.

"So, have you moved back to town?" Alexis asked, desperate to keep Dortman talking.

"Can't trust you not to be recording this," he told her with a harsh laugh. "I took a look at some of the electronic equipment you got in here."

"That's only stuff I use for tutoring students. I just wondered if we'd be staying in town or not. This apartment is pretty small, but you can probably find one nearby."

"You think I'm falling for all this—this sudden change-of-heart crap?"

She had to match his fervor, his anger. He could not think her weak, though she hoped he saw her as being compliant—until she could escape or knock him out.

"Look, Len. You don't think I'm the same person I was after going blind—after living in the dark, where I've done a lot of soul-searching, do you?"

He seemed to have no answer to that. But the fact she'd raised her voice evidently upset Sterling. Instead of just pacing, Alexis could hear her scratching at the bathroom door, something a guide dog would never do. Could she have sensed that her partner was in danger?

"It sounds like my dog needs to go outside—you know, just for a second," she said.

"Oh, right." His voice was mocking as he scooted to the edge of the couch and yanked her to stand beside him. "You think I'm gonna fall for that?"

"Guide dogs are not watchdogs or attack dogs, Len. They're bred to be gentle and calm and to obey orders. If you've been watching me, you've seen that. I hope you'll grow to admire Sterling as much as I do."

For the first time, she could sense Dortman waver. She could almost hear his mind working behind those thick glasses he always wore. And if he still wore them, would it even the playing field if she could get them off his face?

"One thing that's changed for me," she said, fighting back the nausea that began to make her feel even more shaky, "is that I see in many different ways now. With my ears, my hands. Can I just touch your face?"

"So you can try to scratch my eyes out? I'm not really buying any of this, not after the things you done, like getting the cops on my tail. And don't try anything funny, 'cause I got a weapon this time."

A gun or a knife? But he'd had both hands on her. If he was telling the truth, could a weapon be stuck in the waistband of his pants or had he put it down somewhere? But so what? Even if she got her hands on it, she had no clue how to use a gun or a knife without being able to see.

"At least let me feed my dog to quiet her down. She'll get louder and louder if I don't, and that will upset my neighbors." She prayed that he really didn't have a gun—or that he'd be afraid to discharge it.

But she still wanted to let Sterling out of the bathroom. At the very least, the dog seemed to have a calming effect on people. At best, Alexis realized that if she could just make her way into the kitchen, she could get her hands on some sort of weapon.

And the electrical breaker box was there.

Though the lights were out on her floor and in her cell—the officers always turned them out at ten—Tina sat on the floor next to Corky's bed, petting the dog.

Puppies Behind Bars—People Behind Bars. Only

the dogs flourished with the care and love they were given. That's the way it should have been with her kids, Tina thought. She should have been there for them, held them, played with them, raised them up right, not been out at all hours screwing up her life, thinking only of herself. But raising Sterling and Corky showed others and herself that she was capable of more. And despite the mess she'd made of her and her kids' lives, she would cling to that, be proud of that.

Corky was so black that Tina almost couldn't pick her out in the cell, though wan light filtered in through the grate in the door. The dog flopped over, closer, putting her jaw on Tina's knee.

"Sure would like to have you with me for a demo-dog when I start my grooming business in four years, Corky."

How she wished the dog could grasp what she was saying, Tina thought. Sterling and Corky had given her something precious. She wanted to help herself live a better life, and others, too. She'd found hope and purpose working for and with Puppies Behind Bars.

Corky seemed to nod, and put her paw up on Tina's knee as if to say, "That's doggone right."

* * *

Alexis's skin crawled each time Dortman touched her. Now, with his hands so hard on her wrists, she went numb clear down to her fingertips. He shoved her into the hall and banged her into the closed bathroom door.

"You shut that dog up, or I will."

"If you won't let her out to relieve herself, just let me give her one of her treats to calm her down. She's been trained not to bark."

"Oh, yeah? Give her something then, but I'm right behind you, babe, just like the old days, huh? And either of you gets out of line 'fore I get the treat I came for, you'll be real sorry. I'm gonna open that door now, but that dog so much as growls at me, she's a goner."

He did have a gun. He must have a gun.

"I told you, Len, guide dogs are gentle and kind and accepting of strangers. Just let me take her into the kitchen."

When he loosed her left arm, the blood rushed back into her hand, making it prickle. She felt for the knob and opened the door.

"Good girl, Sterling," she crooned, and stooped as

far as Dortman would let her to pat the dog's head. "Everything's all right. Want a treat?"

The Lab, soaking wet, followed Alexis toward the kitchen. Although Dortman let go of her other hand at last, he stayed close to her. Alexis reached in the cupboard for the milk bone, then decided to grab several. She dropped the first one to the floor and heard Sterling devour it. For the first time, she wished the dog were a security dog who would respond to an attack command.

"Can I fix something for you, Len?" she asked, edging past him. "Excuse me, but I just want to get some dog food out of the first cupboard."

"Oh, yeah, bet you'd like to put poison in something for me. And I don't like the way the dog keeps looking at you and then me."

Yes, Alexis thought, this had to work. Because it was going to be her only chance. If she turned off the lights and tried to grab his glasses, she'd have the upper hand. She knew this place in the dark, and he didn't. If he had a gun, it would take him a minute to get it out. She'd call Sterling and flee—if he fired the gun, the sound might summon someone.

"Would you believe my mother got me some

talking cans?" she said, desperate to have him believe she was calm, ready to obey him, when she was prepared to risk her own life to be rid of this man once and for all. Whatever his plans for her, she had to fight back. Having Sterling, trusting Blair—she'd made so many key decisions lately that she suddenly wasn't afraid to make this one.

She hit the button on one of the cans, hoping it would distract him. "Hello, darling," the recording device spoke. "This is applesauce, though you should buy the kind in jars since it tastes much bet—"

Alexis seized the can and heaved it at the spot where she was certain Dortman's face would be. He grunted. Had it hit him? She threw another can, another, then flung herself past him, reaching for the metal cover of the electrical-control box on the wall at the end of the galley kitchen. She slammed it open, yanked down every breaker switch, even as she heard Dortman curse and come after her.

He grabbed her hair and dragged her back. They both went down to their knees. She had to get away from him before he righted himself.

She reached out with both hands to claw at his face and ripped his glasses off. Then he swung a fist at her, hitting her shoulder, and she did what she had been trying so hard not to.

She screamed.

Sterling growled and bumped into her legs. In the scuffle, she felt, then heard Dortman go down on all fours. Was he scrambling for his glasses, or had Sterling tripped him? Alexis vaulted out of the narrow kitchen, but she heard him cursing behind her.

What if he did have a gun? What if he shot Sterling? Was the dog still in the kitchen?

"Sterling, forward! Heel!" she shouted, but she wasn't sure what a dog out of harness would do.

The moment she felt the Lab beside her, she ran for the door, fumbling with the safety chain with one hand, trying to turn the bolt with the other.

She heard Dortman coming. It sounded as if he was bumping into things. He was going to reach her before she got out.

She threw herself back from the door and heard him crash into it. His eyes would adjust to the light seeping in from the street outside. Even without his glasses, he might see her form against the window.

Despite the fact that it would give her position

away, she seized a lamp and threw it at him. It shattered against the door. Trying to keep low so her silhouette wouldn't be outlined by light from the window, she began to heave potted plant after plant at him. Some pots shattered against the wall, others onto the floor, but she was certain more than one hit him. And then she hefted the largest of her plants, the painted stoneware pot, and threw it through the front window, screaming, "Help me. Help me! Help!"

Sterling growled; her big, wet body stuck to her legs like glue. Perhaps the dog was trying to push her back from Dortman. Could he be on the floor?

She knew there could be jagged glass, but she was going through that window!

Yet as she clambered over the couch and got on her knees to lunge toward the opening where cool night air poured in, Sterling placed her solid body against Alexis's knees again, shoving her back onto the couch.

Frenzied, almost hysterical now, Alexis held to the dog's neck, then realized the room had gone silent except for Sterling's panting and her rapid breathing. Had Dortman gone out the back window where he'd come in? Was he hurt but furious, ready to leap on her? Was he just hiding so she'd think he was gone?

Alexis scrambled for the door. The chain was unhooked, so she must have gotten that loose earlier. She turned the safety lock and bolted out into the hall, yelling, "Sterling, heel!"

She heard the dog behind her. From out on the street came male voices, no one she knew.

"Call the police!" she shouted as she made her way outside. "There's a man after me—in my apartment. Tell the police to get Detective Blair Ryan, please—Blair Ryan!"

She heard one of the men make a hurried call as she stumbled down the sidewalk. His voice carried to her as she huddled behind a tree, her arms around Sterling's neck.

"Yeah, 911? There's a woman with her pet dog here and some guy tried to attack her…"

She heard him report the address and ask that they send Detective Blair Ryan. But her Good Samaritan didn't mention that she was blind. All that she'd been through, yet for now, Alexis was just a woman with her dog. A wonderful dog helping her find her way to a wonderful life, she vowed, wiping tears away.

It began to spit rain. Someone draped a raincoat

around her. Sterling kept close to her. A car screeched up, and she heard Blair's voice.

"Alexis!" he cried. She heard him run toward her, but she pointed to her apartment.

"I think Dortman's still inside!"

He almost skidded to a stop, then vaulted past her up the steps.

CHAPTER
~ SIX ~

"Blind Woman Battles Attacker—And Wins." Blair read the newspaper headline to her. "My mother's paper said, Dog Proves To Be Local Woman's Best Friend."

"Or did they mean *loco* woman?" he teased, and she managed to find his shoulder with her fist.

"At least he lied about being armed," she whispered as if to herself.

She'd just gotten off the phone with her mother. Alexis had urged her not to come right now, and no, she wasn't moving home. Nor was she changing apartments again. For now, this was home and Dortman was going to prison. Her comatose attacker, under police guard, had been hauled off to the hospital with a skull fracture—either from a can of applesauce or a potted plant—and from there would be going straight to jail until his indictment and trial.

Blair had offered his apartment for her and Sterling, since hers was both a crime scene and a war zone. But when she had decided to stay here, he'd boarded up her broken window and helped her sweep up shards and strewn potting soil.

"Don't read me the rest of that article," Alexis told Blair, who was leaning in the doorway to the kitchen as she fixed them a tossed salad. "I'm in too good of a mood right now."

"It does mention that you had help from your canine companion. It's good publicity for how well dogs like Sterling are trained. I hope the inmate who raised her gets to read it. You know—'Prison-reared Dog Helps Send Attacker to Jail.' That's the headline I would have used."

"That's it," Alexis said.

"What's it?"

"Let's inquire if we can take Sterling to visit the woman who raised her to thank her and the program for what they do. Sterling helped me by tripping Dortman and she kept me from throwing myself out a broken window, but the fact she remained calm helped me to stay calm—for a while, at least."

Alexis heard the newspaper crinkle, and Blair's arms came warm and strong around her. She stopped washing the broccoli and turned into the circle of his embrace.

"The prison visit's a great idea," he said. "Let's see if we can get permission—if you'll let me go, too."

"I think Sterling would miss you if you didn't."

"And Sterling's partner?" he said, lowering his head to nuzzle her throat.

"Could always use another partner—a human one who has been as faithful as Sterling. All this has made me see—yes, *see*—how much you mean to me. So, of course—" was all she got out before his mouth silenced hers.

As Alexis walked deeper into the prison, the clanging doors behind her seemed to reverberate in her soul. She had not realized what the security would be like here, layers of it. But she was not afraid, and not only because Blair walked by her side. It was the utter lack of fear she sensed in Sterling. In a way, Sterling was coming home.

It had been arranged that they would meet with the entire Puppies Behind Bars class of inmates and their dogs, but first they would have some private time with Tina Clawson, the woman who had raised Sterling. Afterward, Alexis would thank the inmates for rearing dogs for the blind, and Blair had permission from his police department to express their appreciation for the EDCs that served as their bomb-sniffing dogs—and in advance for others they hoped to obtain from the same program.

"Tina has a dog, too," Jeannie Lancer, the PBB instructor, was telling them as they waited for Tina in the classroom. "Not only has she helped the dog, but the dog's helped her. Oh, here they are. Alexis Michaels and Blair Ryan, I would like you to meet Tina Clawson."

Alexis felt Sterling quiver. The dog stood steady because there had been no command, but she obviously was moved to see her raiser. Alexis thrust out her hand to shake Tina's and realized Tina was trembling, too. The moment Tina's palm touched hers, Alexis put Sterling's leash in it, then bent to quickly release the dog from her harness.

"It's okay, Sterling," Alexis said.

She heard the dog's toenails on the concrete floor as she stood on her hind legs to reach up toward Tina. She heard Tina's sobs and "Puppy, puppy, my Sterling, I'm so proud of you. And here's Corky— Blair and Alexis, this is my Corky."

Blair, his voice raspy, too, said, "My sister and I had a beautiful black Lab just like Corky when we were growing up—not as well trained though."

"Corky's going to end up as a great bomb sniffer," Tina said, still evidently choking back tears.

"Those dogs are amazing and make a huge contribution," Blair told her.

Jeannie's voice cut in. "Now I'm going to get out of your way so you three can talk. I'll be right over in the corner catching up on some desk work if you need me."

Alexis squatted down since she could tell Tina was still at Sterling's level. "I guess you heard how Sterling helped me fight off an attacker."

"I hear a lot of bad stuff in here," Tina said, "but I don't get how someone can be so screwed up to stalk and try to harm an innocent person."

"It's no excuse for him," Alexis explained, "but he

was deserted as a child by his mother and—— Tina, are you okay?" she asked when the woman burst into tears.

"Sorry," she said, stifling her sobs. "It's just that my daughter's been sent to a foster home, and no one wants my boy, and I'm scared he'll think I've deserted him. If only I could find my sister Vanessa, she'd take them both, but I'm afraid I'm just going to lose them."

"You need to locate your sister?" Blair asked. "She's run off or what?"

"She had a sort of falling-out with my mama before she died, and Vanessa just took off. She had a good enough job as a nurse's aide, so she's prob'ly back working in a hospital somewhere around."

"Listen, Tina," Blair told her, "I may not have been able to trace the guy who stalked Alexis, but I'd like to take a shot at finding Vanessa, if you can give me a couple of leads. It would be the least I could do for the contribution PBB has made to this nation's security."

"You mean you could try to trace Vanessa online or something like that?"

Alexis reached out and found Tina's shoulder, then gave it a squeeze. "Blair's a police detective. We just didn't want to mention it right away."

"That's okay," Tina cried. "I feel we're on the same team, now that we're raising puppies for bomb sniffers as well as guide dogs. And I couldn't ever thank you enough if you'd try to help me! So——I have a feeling you two are not just together 'cause you caught that guy Sterling helped you nab. It's more than that, right?"

"A lot more," Blair said.

"That makes me happy, just like seeing how good Sterling's doing. You know," Tina said, her voice calmer now, "I'll just bet you could get Sterling to walk Alexis right down the aisle at a wedding."

❧ EPILOGUE ❧

As far as Alexis knew, their wedding today was a first for the PBB program: Sterling actually walked her down the aisle, even though her mother was on the other side to give her away. Alexis sensed Blair's nervousness and happiness as he squeezed her hand, and her mother took Sterling's harness, leaving them standing at the front of the church to face the minister and a new life together.

During the service, Alexis heard the occasional click of cameras. A friend of Blair's was taking wedding pictures for them, and Tina's two kids both had cameras and promised to take the photos to their mother next week when their aunt Vanessa took them to visit her again. Blair had traced Tina's sister through her career as a nurse's aide and found her not far away, working at a seniors' health center. She'd been more than willing to raise both of Tina's kids until Tina was paroled.

The wedding reception was going to be a great reunion. The guest list included some of Alexis's students; Andy Curtis, Sterling's guide dog instructor; and even the police officer, a close friend of Blair's, who was going to train Tina's dog, Corky, to be a bomb sniffer.

Wanting to cherish every moment, Alexis inhaled deeply. She smelled Blair's pine-scented aftershave as he bent close to kiss her, the sweet roses in her bouquet—and everyone's joy. She might be blind, but she could clearly see a lovely, blessed future.

Dear Reader,

I was so impressed by Puppies Behind Bars (PBB) and by meeting Gloria Gilbert Stoga, as well as several of the PBB dogs and their blind or F.B.I. partners, that I have since included working dogs in two other romantic suspense novels. In *The Hiding Place* (available from MIRA Books) and *Deep Down* (available June '09 from MIRA Books) readers will meet great canine companions. Beamer in *The Hiding Place* was greatly inspired by getting to know several of the beautiful Labrador retrievers of the PBB program.

PBB is a charity that makes a difference where the rubber meets the road—or, in this case, where the paws meet the pavement. Take a look at the great Web site for PBB at: www.puppiesbehindbars.com. There you can learn about supporting this outreach through deeds and dollars as it breaks down the barriers of disability, low self-worth and fear.

And despite demands on your time, I would encourage you to get a new "leash on life" by working with charities in your own neighborhood.

Karen Harper

www.karenharperauthor.com